MORGANTOWN PUBLIC LIBRARY
373 SPRUCE STREET
MORGANTOWN, WV 26505

$15.00

MORGANTOWN PUBLIC LIBRARY
373 SPRUCE STREET
MORGANTOWN, WV 26505

1008295

$15.00

8

9 7 8 1 4 6 2 1 1 0 9 8 8

PRAISE FOR

Huber Hill and the Golden Staff of Cíbola

"A fitting conclusion to an epic adventure."
—OBERT SKYE, bestselling author, the Leven Thumps
and the Creature from My Closet series

"*The Golden Staff of Cíbola* is a golden read."
—FRANK L. COLE, bestselling author,
the Hashbrown Winters series

"Parents and educators alike love B. K. Bostick's
books that explore treasured folklore while
taking students on a high-octane adventure kids
just cannot get enough of."
—LAURIE MALINE, elementary school teacher,
North Platte, Nebraska

MORGANTOWN PUBLIC LIBRARY
373 SPRUCE STREET
MORGANTOWN, WV 26505

ALSO BY
B. K. Bostick

Huber Hill and the Dead Man's Treasure
Huber Hill and the Brotherhood of Coronado

MORGANTOWN PUBLIC LIBRARY
373 SPRUCE STREET
MORGANTOWN, WV 26505

HUBER HILL

AND THE

Golden Staff

OF CÍBOLA

MORGANTOWN PUBLIC LIBRARY
373 SPRUCE STREET
MORGANTOWN, WV 26505

HUBER HILL

AND THE

Golden Staff

OF CÍBOLA

B. K. BOSTICK

Sweetwater Books
An Imprint of Cedar Fort, Inc.
Springville Utah

MORGANTOWN PUBLIC LIBRARY
373 SPRUCE STREET
MORGANTOWN, WV 26505

© 2013 B. K. Bostick
All rights reserved.

No part of this book may be reproduced in any form whatsoever, whether by graphic, visual, electronic, film, microfilm, tape recording, or any other means, without prior written permission of the publisher, except in the case of brief passages embodied in critical reviews and articles.

This is a work of fiction. The characters, names, incidents, places, and dialogue are products of the author's imagination, and are not to be construed as real. The opinions and views expressed herein belong solely to the author and do not necessarily represent the opinions or views of Cedar Fort, Inc. Permission for the use of sources, graphics, and photos is also solely the responsibility of the author.

ISBN: 978-1-4621-1098-8

Published by Sweetwater Books, an imprint of Cedar Fort, Inc.,
2373 W. 700 S., Springville, UT 84663
Distributed by Cedar Fort, Inc., www.cedarfort.com

LIBRARY OF CONGRESS CATALOGING-IN-PUBLICATION DATA

Bostick, B. K. (Bryan Keith), 1980- author.
Huber Hill and the Golden Staff of Cibola / by B.K. Bostick.
    pages cm
Summary: Huber, Hannah, and the gang are confronted with a race against time, a madman, and the Brotherhood of Coronado to find the fabled Golden Staff of Cibola.
ISBN 978-1-4621-1098-8 (hardback : alk. paper)
[1. Adventure and adventurers--Fiction. 2. Friendship--Fiction. 3. Gangs--Fiction. 4. New Mexico--Fiction.] I. Title.
PZ7.B649557Hv 2013
[Fic]--dc23
                                        2013017814

Cover illustration by Jerome Jacinto
Cover design by Kelsey Webb
Additional design by Rebecca J. Greenwood
Cover design © 2013 by Lyle Mortimer
Edited and typeset by Melissa J. Caldwell

Printed in the United States of America

10 9 8 7 6 5 4 3 2 1

For my daughter, Lucy Marie
"You make me happy when skies are gray."

MORGANTOWN PUBLIC LIBRARY
373 SPRUCE STREET
MORGANTOWN, WV 26505

MORGANTOWN PUBLIC LIBRARY
373 SPRUCE STREET
MORGANTOWN, WV 26505

PROLOGUE

1539—New Mexico

FRAY MARCOS DE NIZA awaited anxiously. Off in the distance, he made out riders galloping over the hardpan desert. As the riders neared, he recognized their leader, the governor of Galicia, Francisco Vasquez de Coronado. Niza took a breath and steeled himself for what was surely to come. It did not matter what earthly or physical tortures this ruthless man would inflict upon him for his deceit. His soul belonged to a higher power. Niza stepped out of the pueblo onto the path leading outside, clearly visible to Coronado. The riders approached the priest and made a circle around him, making escape impossible. The gesture was unnecessary; he did not plan to escape. Coronado dismounted, kicking up dust as his feet hit the ground. Niza took a breath as the imposing conquistador stepped deliberately toward him. Coronado removed his steel helmet and dropped it.

"I would think a priest to be honest in all his dealings," Coronado sneered.

"What do you mean?" Niza replied, playing dumb. "Did you not find the golden city as I directed?"

"We followed your directions and found tiny villages full of impoverished natives!"

Niza did his best to continue the ruse. "I only saw the city from a distance. I swear to you, it appeared to be made of solid gold. Of course these eyes are getting older . . ."

"Imbecile! Do you have any idea of the resources and manpower you've wasted?"

"My deepest apologies, Your Excellency. My eyes must have deceived me with the setting sun."

"If you were not a man of the church, you would've been hanged by now."

"Governor, I cannot adequately express my regret for my mistake."

Coronado looked down upon the humble priest with disdain. He brought his sallow, bearded face within inches of Niza's. "If I find out you have deliberately deceived me, you won't be able to hide behind those robes. Even the church will not be able to protect you out here in the desert."

Niza nodded emphatically. "Yes, Governor, I understand completely. How shall we proceed?"

Coronado smirked. "I will make the best of a horrid situation." He threw up his hands. "False leads! Defections from my own men seeking riches for themselves! I have claimed this land for Spain, including the villages of the natives you so love. They will work the land for their new governor and I will keep searching the desert until I find cities drowning in riches like Cuzco in the south."

Niza did his best to conceal his dislike for the governor. He had indeed grown fond of the native people he had met during his journeys. He had done his best to protect them from men like Coronado, but despite his best efforts, he may have made things worse. It had been his hope that when Coronado looked upon the humble pueblos, he would simply turn away and head back to Mexico City. How he wished now he had never mentioned the word *Cíbola* to anyone.

Coronado stuck his long finger in Niza's chest. "Perhaps the bigger question is what will you do now to recompense the empire for this disaster?"

"What would you ask of me, Your Excellency?" Coronado smiled and yelled for one of his men to bring the woman. A break opened up in the formation surrounding the two men. One of Coronado's foot soldiers shoved a native Zuni woman through and she fell to her knees in front of them.

Coronado pointed to the woman. "This wretch attacked me when I asked for her necklace. As you know, Fray Marcos, this land and all of its people and possessions now belong to *España*. She has refused to comply with her government and therefore must be executed. You know her language well enough. Tell her what will happen to her." He grinned sadistically.

Niza's eyes implored the Governor. "Please, Your Excellency. In your mercy, could you not forgive such a trespass? She likely mistook you for invaders. In time, she will come to see you as a benevolent leader and governor."

"Her fate is sealed. Now do your duty."

Niza frowned. "Yes, Governor."

Coronado then whistled for one of his men to accompany Niza out into the brush where the execution would take place. The priest picked the woman up by the arm and escorted her toward certain demise. Coronado's solider walked on the other side of the woman.

Speaking in her native tongue, the priest began conversing. "What is your name?"

"Sunitha," the woman replied.

"Listen closely," Niza said. "The man accompanying us intends to put an end to your life."

"I know," she replied curtly.

Their escort made no effort to listen in, unable to understand the words spoken. Niza continued, "When we get to the brush, I will distract the executioner. When I do, run and take this with you." The priest slipped something into the pocket of Sunitha's garment.

"What is this?"

"My diary. It must never fall into the wrong hands. It contains directions and clues to find the actual golden city of Cíbola. Have you been there?"

"No," the woman replied. "I have heard stories that a branch of my kin lived there many years ago. I've seen trinkets from the golden city, but none of my people have ever seen it with their own eyes. Are you saying you've seen the city?"

"Yes, and more than seen. I was led there by my companion, Esteban, months ago. We entered the city. I have never seen anything so glorious. My tongue was too loose, and the governor heard of our journey. He demanded I take him there, so I purposely led Coronado away from it to your village. I am sorry for what I brought upon you, but I feared what would become of the world if this man were to possess the city and the power that lies within."

"You speak of the Golden Staff," she said, without making eye contact.

"Yes." The priest nodded. "I found him, the golden king El Dorado. I saw his staff with my own eyes."

"And you did not attempt to take it for yourself?"

"Such power should never belong to a single person. The object is wicked."

"On that we agree," the woman said. She still had

not made eye contact with the priest. "What happened to your friend, Esteban?"

The priest sighed and didn't answer.

"Your friend is dead," she said, somehow knowing.

The priest hung his head. "He and all our company. Between ambushes along the way and the city's hidden traps, I was the only one who survived. Divine Providence perhaps," he said. "My diary chronicles our journey and how to navigate the way into the city's center—to Dorado."

"What shall I do with these writings?"

"Keep them, burn them—just get them away from Coronado and his men."

"I will honor your request should I survive."

"You will survive. I will see to it."

They had ventured beyond the pueblo a fair distance into the brush. The executioner motioned for the woman to get down on her knees and then extracted his sword.

"Fray Marcos." The soldier motioned toward the Bible attached to the priest's hip.

"Oh yes." He withdrew the holy book and opened it to a passage located in Proverbs. He read solemnly, "How much better is it to get wisdom than gold! and to get understanding rather to be chosen than silver! The high-way of the upright is to depart from evil: *she* that keepeth *her* way"—the priest winked at the woman—"preserveth *her* soul."

As he finished his sentence, the priest pounced upon

the soldier, tackling him to the ground. Sunitha was instantly on her feet and running through the brush. She had a good head start before the soldier shouted to his comrades that their captive was escaping. Niza and the executioner wrestled in the dirt before the priest was overcome. Coronado and his men on horseback were soon at the site of confrontation.

"The woman is getting away!" one of the men cried.

"Let her go!" Coronado shouted as he rode up to Niza, who was now constrained. "Foolish move, my righteous friend."

"What shall we do with the priest?" the same man asked.

"Death would be too easy," the Governor said. "He shall return to Mexico City in shame. All will know of his folly. He will be mocked and spat upon in the streets. He will die lonely and desolate, just like this desert where he has led us."

Niza said nothing but mustered the courage to meet Coronado's gaze.

Just then a rider broke into the group and interrupted them. He was anxious and out of breath. "Your Excellency! I've found something that warrants your attention!"

"What is it?" Coronado snapped.

The rider retrieved something from his satchel. It was a thin tablet that had the appearance of gold. On its face were strange markings and symbols. "While raiding the pueblo, I found this in one of the elders' homes. He claims it contains directions to a city full of riches beyond imagination! He claims it leads to the *real* city of Cíbola!"

Coronado snatched the thin golden tablet, then looked down upon the priest. "So . . . it appears there is a city of gold after all, Priest. Whether you led us here in deception or by stupidity, it matters not, Fray Marcos. I will find the golden city of Cíbola." He then turned toward the rider who had brought him the prize. "Bring me the elder and have him translate this language!"

The rider's face fell. "I'm sorry, Your Excellency. I attempted to have the man translate, but he claims there are but few who can decipher that dialect of Zuni language due to its age."

"Niza!" Coronado boomed. "You know their language. Translate the thing!"

The soldier brought the tablet before Niza.

The priest looked it over and shook his head. "I apologize, Your Excellency, but this writing goes beyond my knowledge as well. I cannot help you."

"Then who can?" the Governor demanded.

Just then, another of Coronado's soldiers galloped toward the group. "Good news!" the man shouted. "I found a villager that knows who can translate the language! The woman Sunitha can help us. Is she not the one we took captive? Where is she?"

Coronado's eyes smoldered with anger. He withdrew

his sword and pointed it at the priest's chest, then raised it toward the desert. "Find her!"

In a flurry of dust, the horsemen galloped past Niza into the desert. They'd never find her. The sun had just disappeared behind the horizon, and soon night would cover the woman's tracks.

As Coronado bolted forward, he kicked Niza in the chest and sent him sprawling to the ground. Over his shoulder, the governor shouted, "Pray we never meet again, Priest! And pray for the woman should we find her! Cíbola belongs to me, Fray Marcos! *I will fill my cup!*"

HUBER INVOLUNTARILY GRIMACED AS the vehicle's headlights lit up a green sign—*Welcome to Carbondale*. For several days, Huber, Hannah, Scott, and Eagle Claw had been racing toward Colorado in a rented car they'd picked up in Virginia. Carlos, Pincho, Alejandro, and Yesenia—or Jessie as she liked to be called—had gone onto New Mexico to try to find Malia's family and inform them of what had happened to her in Spain. They hoped to outrace Juan Hernán Salazar and his companion to the area.

Huber and the others would catch up with them after stopping in Carbondale to look for any clues regarding the disappearance of their parents. It had been a long couple of weeks. The adventure overseas was one Huber ordinarily would've enjoyed. To avoid capture by the

Brotherhood of Coronado, they'd taken a boat across the Atlantic. The endless horizons, sightings of whales, and spray of salty mist in the morning couldn't distract his thoughts from his parents. Shortly after embarkation, Jessie had received a message from the Brotherhood of Coronado on her cell phone—*Such is the fate of all who cross the Brotherhood*, it had said. Beneath the message was a picture of Huber's and Scott's parents, blindfolded and bound. Since that time, thoughts of Cíbola, gold, or even things like food had fallen to the wayside. Huber had to help his parents.

One thing that had been effective in helping Huber pass the time during his trip overseas was Don Carlos. The old man and master fencer had taken to teaching Huber the basics of sword fighting. On the deck of the ship, they'd set up straw dummies, and Huber had taken to the sport fairly quickly. Carlos told him that practicing on a moving ship would assist in his balance. Melee combat would not be a bad skill to have in case Huber ran into Salazar or members of the Brotherhood of Coronado.

Just over a month ago, Huber and his companions had traveled to Spain and confronted the Brotherhood of Coronado, a secret organization bent on locating and stealing the lost treasures of the world to finance their ultimate goal—a new world order, led by the Brotherhood and their three kings: Susurro and Matón, the two lesser kings; and Fausto, their leader.

"Finally here," Huber said to his sister, who brushed her blonde hair out of her eyes.

"Feels like it's been forever," she said.

"What time is it?" Scott stirred next to her from a restless sleep.

"Close to midnight," Huber answered. "We're back in Carbondale."

"Midnight? McDonald's should still be open then. I'm starving. How 'bout we go there first and grab some Big Macs? I'd even eat one of those Filet O' Fish things."

Scott had tried to keep up his humor, but his father had also been taken by the Brotherhood. Huber could tell the abduction occupied his every thought. The humor was a mask, a distraction from what was happening inside.

"Where to first?" Eagle Claw asked from the driver's seat. "And I'm not going to McDonald's."

"Our house is closest," Huber said. "Let's go there first. Then we can go to Scott's."

Eagle Claw, a member of the Ute tribe, had shown up in Spain to help rescue Huber and his friends from the Brotherhood. He was the mighty son of Hawk, an old friend who had been assassinated by the Brotherhood for trying to protect a treasure—the Dead Man's Treasure—in the mountains near Huber's hometown. The Brotherhood had prevailed over its protectors and taken the treasure with them to Spain.

From the passenger seat, Huber directed Eagle Claw

through the town's side streets toward their home. A few minutes later, the car rolled to the front-side curb. The lights to his house were out. Huber instantly homed in on the pink flamingo in his yard, placid and hideous as ever.

"Well, we're home."

"I'll go in first," Eagle Claw volunteered. "Do you have a key?"

"It's inside that fake rock next to the flamingo," Hannah said, pointing.

"Wait five minutes. If I don't come back out, call the police and do not come inside. If the house is safe, I'll motion for you to follow. Understood?"

Huber's stomach tightened as he nodded. He'd been anticipating this moment for several days. The Brotherhood may have known they'd come back here. Who knew what surprises could be waiting inside?

Eagle Claw exited the car and stealthily made his way toward the front door. He quickly found the fake rock and retrieved the key. Seconds later, he disappeared through the front door.

Huber exhaled. "Well, he's inside."

"How come he ain't turnin' on the lights?" Scott asked.

"Not sure," Huber said. "Maybe he's making sure no one's inside first."

The seconds ticked away like bomb bursts.

"He should've been back out by now," Hannah said, her voice quickening. "Let's go call the cops."

"Heck with that," Scott said, opening the backseat door next to Hannah. "I'm goin' inside."

"Scott! What are you doing?"

"These guys got my dad too, remember? If we call the cops, the Brotherhood'll find out somehow. What d'ya think'll happen to our folks then?"

Before she could answer, Scott was out of the car, jogging toward the front door to the Hill household. The black doorway swallowed him up.

"What should we do?" Hannah asked her brother.

Huber shot her a glance through the rearview mirror and, without saying anything, exited the car. Hannah followed suit.

Huber's feet floated over the walkway. The front door was still slightly ajar. Hannah was closely behind. There were no sounds coming from the house.

"Be careful," she whispered.

Huber pushed the door open and stepped inside. Faint light filtered through the front room windows. Everything seemed undisturbed, just as he'd left it before traveling to Spain over a month ago.

He had received an invitation to travel there from Jessie, a girl who claimed to know what had happened to the Dead Man's Treasure. She claimed it had been stolen by the Brotherhood of Coronado. With their spoils, they planned to organize power and discover the ultimate treasure, the fabled Golden Staff of Cíbola. From what Huber could remember of the ancient story, a lowly Zuni villager named Lonan was given the staff from a demon named Uhepono. The staff, the demon informed the villager, would make him more powerful than any man on earth because it granted him the ability to turn anything he touched with its amber tip to gold. Lonan greedily accepted the staff and turned his entire city, Cíbola, into a shimmering city of solid gold. Not surprisingly, the power corrupted him, and he ultimately turned the staff on his fellow villagers and himself, changing everyone to golden statues.

Upon hearing the fantastic stories from Zuni natives, the Spanish referred to Lonan as *El Dorado*, the "Golden One," and Cíbola as the Golden City. One ambitious conquistador, Francisco Coronado, spent years searching for Cíbola in vain. The Brotherhood planned to finish what Coronado had started.

After arriving in Spain to take on the Brotherhood, Huber had been captured and met a fellow captive named Malia. The Brotherhood had abducted this young Zuni girl due to her rare ability to translate her tribe's ancient dialect of language. The Three Kings of the Brotherhood wanted her to translate a golden tablet they'd acquired, supposedly written by El Dorado himself, describing how to find his city of gold. The Brotherhood, however, had been duped by Jessie and her grandfather, Carlos, who infiltrated the Brotherhood's castle, stole the real tablet, and replaced it with a forgery.

In the end, however, it was Huber and his friends who had truly been fooled. Juan Hernán Salazar, an old enemy masked as an ally, had used Huber and his friends as a distraction to get what he really wanted: the genuine tablet written by El Dorado, and Malia to translate it. With it, he hoped to find the staff, use it to destroy the Brotherhood, and become the richest man on earth.

On the bright side, they had recovered the Dead Man's Treasure from the Brotherhood, which was the original goal of their trip. Eagle Claw had already put plans in motion to return the treasure to its original mountain resting place deep inside an abandoned Spanish mine. However, the victory seemed hollow when they considered the scheme they'd uncovered by the Brotherhood. Huber shuddered at the thought of allowing the Golden Staff of Cíbola to fall into their hands. Of course, Huber had not yet fully bought into the story that such an object actually existed. Nonetheless, the Brotherhood was convinced, and Huber couldn't take the chance.

From the backyard, Huber could hear his dog, Hobo, barking. He wondered who had been taking care of the mangy thing.

He flipped the light switch but nothing happened.

"Power is out," he said to his sister.

"The lights were on at the Nielsens' next door."

"This isn't good. Someone must've cut it."

"Scott? Eagle Claw?" Huber shouted from the doorway, ready to bolt back outside.

No answer came.

"Something's wrong. C'mon, let's head to the Nielsens'."

"What's the hurry?" a deep, gruff voice said from somewhere in the darkness. The voice carried a Spanish accent. Huber instantly recognized it. The voice belonged to Matón, or King Crusher, one of the lesser kings of the Brotherhood of Coronado. Huber had first met the brute in an alleyway in Spain. His frame had towered over everyone else, his bulging muscles almost ripping through his clothing. His fists had been gloved in some kind of mechanics, lending further strength to his terrific blows. Huber shuddered as he recalled the man punching through solid brick walls back in Spain. Now this monster was in his house.

Huber started and looked to his left. Matón was sitting in his mother's glider, gently rocking, his face obscured by shadow.

"What are you doing here?" Huber trembled. "Where are my parents?"

"Where do you think they are?" he said and stood. "*La inquisición.*" He chuckled.

Huber's hands quaked as he remembered his own inquisition at the hands of the Brotherhood within their castle in Spain. The three kings had placed him on a glowing diode in the floor, demanding answers to questions. As he answered incorrectly or spoke out of turn, he had received powerful shocks through his feet, which filled his entire body with the worst pain he'd ever endured. Huber thought of his parents receiving similar treatment. His fear turned to anger.

Matón stepped from the obscure corner of the room, and the streetlight from outside reflected off his silver-covered face. The expression etched in the mask was just as Huber remembered, a tense grimace meant to intimidate. The fitted black clothing he wore hid his beefy form and created the illusion of a silver face floating in the dark. He donned no ceremonial helmet as he had in the Spanish castle. His long hair fell behind his shoulders in a ponytail. "Huber," the king said. "I've been waiting here for some time."

"Where's Eagle Claw and Scott?"

Matón snapped his fingers, causing his mechanical gloves to whine, and several flashlights clicked on across the room. Huber saw Scott and Eagle Claw, gagged and subdued by Brotherhood goons.

Hannah gasped. "Let them go! What do you want?"

"I think you know what we want, young one. Where is the Zuni girl? Where is El Dorado's tablet you stole from us?"

"Gone," Hannah said. "Juan Hernán Salazar took her and the tablet before we came back to America, I swear it!"

"Lies," he hissed.

Eagle Claw and Scott yelled through their gags as the foot soldiers dragged them off toward the kitchen area. The soldiers' faces were covered in mesh and their clothing was black as night.

"She's telling the truth!" Huber yelled. "Don't hurt them!"

Matón tramped forward. "I won't hurt them, Huber. They and your parents will go free. We will walk away from here as if nothing ever happened. You have my word. All we want in return is the girl and the tablet."

More struggling sounded from the kitchen.

"What are they doing to them?" Hannah's chest rose in panic.

Matón cocked his head toward the kitchen in the semi darkness, then back toward the twin siblings. His gargantuan presence seemed a terrible nightmare.

"You have ten seconds to tell me before my men do *permanent* damage to your friends."

"We're telling the truth!" Huber reiterated. "I promise you!"

Matón stepped forward, punching one mighty fist into the other.

"And *I* promise you will tell me the truth when I'm through with you."

Suddenly, a large figure tackled the king from the shadows. In the darkness, Huber made out Eagle Claw squeezing Matón's mechanical fists until they began to smoke. It was a battle of titans, Eagle Claw just a few inches shorter than Matón's seven feet and a few pounds less in stature. The lesser king of the Brotherhood brought a swift foot out and connected with the back of Eagle Claw's thigh, causing him to stumble. As the king did, he knocked Eagle Claw in the chest with his right fist, the left hand still smoking. Eagle Claw shot backward onto the Hills' coffee table. The table splintered into a thousand pieces under Eagle Claw's weight. Matón lunged forward, and Eagle Claw caught him and then used his momentum to catapult the king backward. The brute smashed into the TV hanging on the wall. The screen cracked like a spider web and fell to the floor. Eagle Claw struggled to his feet.

"I've been waiting for this," Matón wheezed. "Last time we met in the castle, I remember you shooting a dart in my neck before we could have a fair fight."

Huber recalled Eagle Claw and his friends coming to his rescue just before the Brotherhood was about to dispatch him in a sick game of chance.

Eagle Claw also gasped for air. "Fair fight? You're the one using those machines for fists. Afraid your own strength can't do the job?"

Matón growled and fiddled with the strength enhancements. The left glove, still slightly smoking, fell to the ground. The right followed suit. He held up his bare knuckles and extended his sausage-like fingers. "I won't need them for the likes of you."

"Sure about that?" Eagle Claw grinned. "Perhaps the fight was more fair before." He turned toward Huber and Hannah. "Go ahead and get out of here," he said, never allowing his eyes to leave Matón.

A car horn blared from outside.

"Scott is in the car waiting for you," Eagle Claw continued. "I'll catch up. Run before the men I knocked unconscious awaken!"

Matón made a guttural sound, rested his chin on his knuckles, and used them to snap his neck backward, making a sick, crackling sound.

"Ahh, *mejor*," he whispered. "Let's go, big man. You won't get so lucky again."

"Go!" Eagle Claw repeated as he charged forward toward Matón.

"C'mon, Huber!" Hannah pulled her brother toward the front door.

Huber forced himself forward through the door, not allowing his eyes to avert from the idling car where Scott sat behind the wheel. The bangs and crashes continued inside the house. Hannah jumped in the backseat and Huber rode shotgun.

"I don't know what's more dangerous," Hannah said to Scott. "You behind the wheel or taking my chances back inside with that giant!"

"What about Eagle Claw?" Huber asked. "Can we really leave him here?"

"He told me to drive to Roswell, New Mexico, and to not look back. That's where he said we'll meet up with Carlos and the others," Scott said.

Huber could still see colossal shadows wrestling through his front room window. "I hope he makes it."

"Of course he'll make it," Scott said. "You shoulda seen 'im take out those Brotherhood dudes. He threw 'em around like they were rag dolls. I'm guessin' there's no need to stop by my place, is there? Who knows what's waitin' there. Next stop, New Mexico."

Scott threw the car into gear and flew backward, smashing the Hills' garbage bin.

"Oops. Better buckle up for safety."

"Yeah, and pray like there's no tomorrow," Hannah added.

THEY'D BEEN DRIVING FOR hours on Highway 285. The dawn had given birth to mountainous green, which gradually gave way to sagebrushed desert, then Joshua trees. They'd stopped to fill up once along the way, not long after they'd passed the sign with a sun symbol welcoming them to "The Land of Enchantment"—New Mexico. Huber tried to relax, sitting in the seat next to Scott, but he was worried about Eagle Claw. Sleep came in intermittent fits. They had just passed through Santa Fe when Scott glanced in the rearview mirror and sighed.

"Uh-oh," he said.

"What's wrong?" Huber asked.

"See for yourself." He glanced behind his shoulder.

Huber's stomach dropped. Red, blue, and white lights flashed behind them. A siren signaled for them to pull over. "Scott! Were you speeding?"

"Just a little," Scott said, trying to sound innocent. "Only like twenty miles per hour over though."

Huber sighed.

"What do we do?" Hannah shouted from the back seat. "What's going to happen when he asks for your license?"

"Don't worry," Scott said confidently. "Got it covered."

"That's reassuring." She rolled her eyes.

Huber tried to think fast. "It wouldn't do us any good to try and outrun him in a Kia."

"I could try." Scott grinned and flitted his eyebrows. "This one seems to have some guts in her."

"Don't!" Huber and Hannah said in unison.

"Fine, I'll pull over. Just leave the talkin' to me. I've got myself out of lots of jams like this before."

"Why am I not surprised?" Hannah shook her head.

Scott pulled the car to the side of the road. Huber watched through the rear windshield as a highway patrol woman stepped from the patrol car. She had short, spiky dark hair and thick, black sunglasses. Scott unrolled his window and smiled up at the officer as she approached. The sun filtered through his short red hair and caused him to squint up at the woman.

"Wow!" he said to her as she stood before him. "Are you gonna give me a ticket? Cuz you've got *FINE* written all over you. Seriously, someone oughta call the cops on you 'cuz it should be illegal to be so beautiful. Honestly, feel free to pull me over anytime."

Huber groaned and put his face in his hands. This was not going to end well. If Scott was trying to charm the patrol woman, it didn't seem to be working. She didn't even show the faintest hint of being amused.

"You kids were driving pretty fast back there," she said, glancing from Scott to Huber to Hannah. "About twenty miles per hour over the limit fast."

"I'm real sorry," Scott replied. "If I'd known you were hiding behind that sign, I woulda slowed down, I promise."

The patrol woman shot him a menacing glance. "Can I see your license, young man?"

"Sure," Scott said and pulled out his wallet. He fiddled through it and handed her a card with his picture on it.

"This is a school lunch ID." The officer raised a brow behind her sunglasses. "How old are you?"

"Old enough," Scott said with a half smile.

The officer's demeanor didn't crack even a little. "Am I to assume you're driving without a license?"

Scott flipped through his wallet compartments. "That was just a joke. Here's my license," he said, handing her another card.

The officer glanced at it. "You're from New Hampshire, are you? Mr. Abraham Nowinski?"

"That's correct," Scott said. "People just call me Abe, though. I'm here visiting my cousins."

"The plates on this car are from Virginia," the officer

observed. "And this license looks about as phony as a three-dollar bill."

Huber held his breath. They were surely caught now.

"That's right. This car is a rental. My parents and I flew in from New Hampshire to pick up my aunt Vickie. From there we drove here to visit my other aunt and uncle, Dorris and Ned. It's a family reunion of sorts."

"So where are your parents?"

"Santa Fe," Hannah answered for Scott.

Huber couldn't believe it. Now his sister was joining in on the lies.

"This is my brother, Daniel." Hannah pointed to Huber. "Like Abe said, he and his folks are visiting us."

"And may I ask your name?" the officer said.

"Lucy . . . Nowinski," she said unconvincingly.

The officer removed her sunglasses and glanced at Huber. She must've noticed he looked nervous. He averted his eyes and could feel the heat rising from his face.

"You're pretty quiet there, Daniel. Why are you all out here driving alone without your parents?"

Scott and Hannah both looked at Huber. He could tell from the look on their faces they were worried and pleading for him to play along. Huber was not a very good liar. Their eyes implored for him to come up with something.

"Um . . . ," he hemmed and hawed. "I . . ." Then a memory of a billboard they'd passed came to mind. "We're going to Carlsbad Caverns," he said. "Our parents didn't want to go, so Abe just decided to take us. Lucy and I have never been."

"Carlsbad Caverns?" the officer repeated.

Huber, Scott, and Hannah all nodded emphatically.

The officer's face was stoic, her expression giving no hint to what thoughts rolled around in her brain. Finally, her lips parted into a slight grin. "I've loved Carlsbad Caverns since I was a little girl. I was a junior ranger there, you know? I roamed those caves and caverns every summer all day, every day. You're in for a real treat."

They all smiled. Hannah and Scott gave a slight nod to Huber for thinking of the story so quickly.

The officer continued, "Well, I can't blame you for being in a hurry to get down there, but please slow down, okay?"

"Will do, ma'am." Scott smiled and saluted. "Thanks for not givin' us a ticket."

The woman's smile disappeared. "Oh, who said anything about not giving you a ticket?"

They were finished! Huber tried to control his panic. As soon as the patrol woman ran the car's registration and Scott's phony license, there was no way they'd get out of this. Huber imagined himself going to juvie. All of the hardened criminal kids would eat him alive. Scott, on the other hand, would probably fit right in.

"Please hand over the car's registration," she continued.

Huber shakily opened the glove box and retrieved the

car rental's registration. He handed the paper to Scott, who slid it into the woman's hand.

"I'll be right back. Please stay in the car."

The patrolwoman walked back to her vehicle and stepped inside to run the numbers through the computer's database.

"What do we do now?" Hannah quaked. "We're busted."

"I dunno," Scott lamented. "I'm outta ideas. We'll probably be arrested and the car will be impounded. Man, I really don't wanna go to prison. I ain't built for that kinda thing."

"Our parents are still being held captive," Hannah moaned. "We'll be stuck in kid jail and there will be no one to bail us out. Who knows how long we'll be there."

"We can't afford to be arrested," Huber said in surprisingly calm tone. "We need to find our parents and stop the Brotherhood and Salazar from finding Cíbola."

"What do ya suggest then, Huber? Take out the fuzz?" Scott whispered, then pondered the idea. "I like it."

"No, that would be insane. Listen close. We don't have much time. Look out my window, what do you see?"

"Cactus, hills, and lots of brush," Hannah said.

"Exactly. Lots of places to hide."

"You can't be serious, Huber. There's no way we can outrun a police officer. What if she shoots us?"

"She's not going to shoot kids," Huber tried to assure them and himself.

"Might tase us though," Scott said thoughtfully.

"We'll make a run for it and try to hide out, then we can hitch a ride or something to Roswell."

"I don't know, Huber," Hannah cautioned.

"No time to argue. We need to run now while she's not paying attention."

Collectively, the trio looked back at the patrol car. The officer's head was down, staring at her computer.

"Now or never," Huber said.

Scott and Hannah nodded. Huber opened the passenger door and bolted as fast as he could off to the side of the road. He didn't look back, but he could hear Scott and Hannah's footsteps behind him. Huber had never been a particularly fast runner, but the thought of going to juvie livened his steps.

"We're so toast! I never thought I'd be part of a police chase!" he heard Hannah yell from behind.

"Just don't stop!" Scott boomed. "Book it past that bluff!"

Huber scanned ahead. Maybe a hundred yards away was a small drop-off where they'd hopefully disappear from view. Forcing himself to go just a bit faster, Huber reached the bluff and slid downward. The drop was steeper than he anticipated, and suddenly it was like his body was inside a washing machine. Dirt and wild grass flew in his face. He felt prickly sensations now and then. Finally the world became still as he stared up at a bluish-orange sky. Moments later, Hannah and Scott slid to a stop beside him.

"Holy cow, dude!" Scott gasped as he looked at him. "That was a wicked spill! If we coulda filmed that, it would get like a million hits on YouTube! Awesome! Ya okay?"

His world still spinning, Huber looked up at him. "A little help, please."

Scott pulled Huber to his feet. At least nothing felt broken, but as the adrenaline wore away, a burning, painful sensation radiated from his back.

"My back," Huber complained. "It's on fire!"

"Turn around," Hannah said.

He did so and heard her gasp.

"What?"

Scott began to laugh and yanked out a cactus spine. "Ha! Ya look like a hedgehog from this angle!"

"Ouuucch!" Huber winced as he yanked out another. "How many are there?"

"Only about two hundred more to go." Scott laughed.

"We better get a move on before we get caught. The officer won't be far behind," Hannah suggested. "Once we're safe, we'll pull the rest of them out. Can you make it?"

Huber nodded, in too much pain to speak.

"Look! Over there!" Scott pointed.

Concealed behind some scrub oak and cacti was a small grotto carved into the sandstone by time and water. There were some soda cans and charred remains of a fire inside, but they looked to be at least a few days old. Once inside the vacant depression, they wouldn't be visible from the top of the bluff.

They all made their way inside, and from up above, they heard the voice of the officer as she spoke into her radio. "That's right, Joe. At mile marker thirteen. Three runners, ages fourteen or fifteen, I'd say. Kid tried to give me some fake ID. Abandoned their vehicle and fled on foot into the brush."

Inaudible chattering came through the other side before she buzzed back.

"Yes, bring the dogs. Their scent is still fresh in the car. They won't have made it very far. We'll find them quickly."

Once they were confident the officer was out of earshot, Scott finally spoke.

"What we gonna do now? Ain't no outrunnin' police dogs. They'll find us in about ten seconds."

"I don't know." Huber winced, his back still searing. "But we better not stay here long."

"Maybe I can help you out," a deep voice said, startling them.

In unison, their heads popped up and stared at the disheveled man who had been sitting in the shadows of the grotto. He was dressed in rags and a beanie cap, and a long beard adorned a dirty face, tanned and cracked by the New Mexican sun. The man was obviously a vagabond.

"What do you mean?" Huber asked. "How could you help?"

"Overheard everything that's been happening. This is my place," he said. "Normally, I wouldn't mind if I had guests, but I'd just as soon not have the police down here snooping around and kicking me out of my place. Catch my drift?"

"What should we do?" Hannah asked.

"See over there?" The man pointed outside the grotto. "Those tracks? A train is going to pass through here any minute. If you don't want to get caught, you need to be on it."

Huber saw the train tracks he was talking about. They were only a few hundred feet from where they were hiding.

"How are we supposed to jump onto a movin' train?" Scott shook his head.

"It always slows down in this area. How do you think I got here? There should be an empty box car toward the end. Problem is you won't have time to get to it when the train slows. You'll need to jump on one of the other cars and make your way back."

"Sounds pretty dangerous," Huber said.

"So am I if you choose to stay here," he growled. "You decide."

"We'll take the train," Hannah said without hesitation. "Sorry to have invaded your space." She turned to Huber and Scott. "Let's go."

As she finished her sentence, the ground beneath them began to vibrate. From around the bend, a locomotive appeared.

The man continued, "Once the locomotive passes where we are, make a run for it and hope the conductor doesn't see you. Get ready . . ."

The locomotive thudded past their position.

"Now! Now! Get outta here!" he shouted, giving Scott a shove. "And don't come back!"

"Wait! Where does the train go?" Huber yelled above the train's engines.

"Where do you think? Somewhere other than here! Roswell is the next stop!"

That sealed the deal. Not only would the train help them escape the police, but it would also take them to their desired destination. Like bullets, Huber and the others shot out of the grotto toward the train. It still seemed to be going far too fast to board. As they neared, just as the homeless man had said, it began to slow to around five miles per hour. Scott was the first to take a leap. He grabbed onto the side of a tank car full of petroleum. Hannah ran forward and jumped on as well. Scott clutched her arm and pulled her to more steady ground. Still winded and wounded from his earlier sprint, Huber lagged behind. As he approached the tank car, the train began to accelerate again, inching ahead of him.

"C'mon, Huber! Run faster!" Scott yelled. "Quit bein' a wimp and run!"

Huber's legs were two awkward, galloping popsicle sticks. There was no way he was going to make it.

"Huber, unless you want to go to juvie or spend the night with that homeless guy back there, run faster!" Hannah shouted.

Huber pushed harder, but so did the train. Scott reached out as far as he could. Huber lunged forward but barely missed his hand and nearly fell on his face.

"Huber!" His sister shook her head. Her face then brightened. "Jessie is in Roswell!"

The words were magic. While he couldn't call Jessie his girlfriend, she was the closest thing he'd ever had to one, and the thought of seeing her quickened his pace. Suddenly his legs found renewed strength as he pumped them for all he was worth. He gained a few feet toward Scott's outreached hand and leaped forward. His hand struck Scott's at just the right moment. Scott pulled him forward, but the train was still going faster than his legs. It was as if the ground and train were stretching him apart. He groaned, pushed forward, and then slipped completely. His feet were now dragging behind him, bouncing off the ties like mud flaps, each bounce smarting worse than the one before. Mustering what little strength he had left, he pushed off as hard as he could when his feet found traction. It was just enough for Scott to pull him aboard.

The next part of their task was to make their way to the back of the train. The wind howled over Huber's ears and he could barely understand what Scott was saying. Something about climbing to the top of the train and making their way back. There was a small ladder inching up to the top of the fuel car. Scott went first, followed by Hannah. Huber slowly made his way up. As his face crested the top of the car, the wind about took his head off. The train was almost up to full speed now. Making their way to the end of the train wasn't going to be easy with so much friction.

Huber watched Hannah and Scott get down on their bellies.

"It's easier if you crawl!" Hannah shouted over the noise of the iron beast.

Shuffling on his stomach like a snake, Huber followed his companions. At least the adrenaline washed away some of the pain in his back. As they reached the end of the first fuel car, Huber realized they had a problem. There was about a three-foot gap between them and the next car, with no ladder to assist them.

"Gonna hafta jump!" Scott shouted and rose up off his knees.

As he arose, the wind caught him and pushed him forward. His arms flew around like propellers as he attempted to balance his body. Huber grimaced, imagining his best friend toppling off the train going fifty miles per hour. It was like being on a roller coaster with no constraints. Luckily, Scott regained his footing and crouched low to the train. With mixed awe and horror, Huber watched as Scott jumped with the wind and catapulted himself over to the next car, finishing his landing with surprising poise and balance.

Hannah went next and also did fairly well with her jump, but stumbled a bit as she landed. Scott was there to steady her. Now it was Huber's turn. He pushed himself to his feet. As he did, the wind hit his back like a hammer. He had no idea how he'd make the jump, let alone just stay standing. He took a deep breath and sprinted forward. As he jumped, his foot slipped, and he spilled forward face-first into the adjoining fuel car. He looked down and saw the gravel and railroad ties speeding beneath him and wondered why he hadn't crashed into them and been dismembered. He peered upward and saw that Scott had one hand and his sister the other. Together they pulled him on top of the car.

"Thanks!" Huber gasped. "Thought I was roadkill . . . or rail-kill, I guess!"

"You're welcome," Hannah said.

"Sure thing." Scott slapped him on the back. "Only ten more cars to go!"

● ● ●

Huber vaguely remembered making his way toward the back of the train. Jumping the cars had exhausted him to the point of being delirious. The adrenaline kick from almost dying on the first jump must have given him extra strength to make it the rest of the way. They'd found their way into one of the unlocked, empty boxcars at the tail end of the line. His body was so fatigued that he could barely stand. The cactus spines were still stinging his back, but without tweezers, there was no way Hannah could pull them out. At least the trio was safe from the cops. He couldn't sit or lie on his back, so he lay on his stomach, enduring the long, bumpy ride toward Roswell. Two hours later, the train decelerated.

"I think we're here!" Hannah said.

As the train stopped, they filed out of the car into the train depot, skulking low to the ground just in case any employees were around. The night was pitch black and millions of stars shone overhead. The air was chilly and dry.

Once they were a safe distance from the depot, Hannah pulled out her cell phone. "Yes! There's service!"

She dialed a number. An inaudible but clearly worried voice sounded from the other end.

"Yes, we finally made it. You'll have to come pick us up

near the train depot. We lost the car. Had some problems. Eagle Claw isn't with us. We'll tell you about it when you get here. We'll meet you out in front of the station. Please hurry!"

She hung up the phone. "They're on their way to pick us up."

AFTER PINCHO PICKED THEM up at the Roswell
Train Depot, they traveled to a Best Western Inn where
everyone was staying. Apparently, Carlos had rented out
several connecting rooms and was using the motel as a
headquarters of sorts. He had set up shop in a room of his
own, filling it with books, supplies, maps, and everything
an Antarctic expedition might need. The boys would stay
in one room, the girls in another. Carlos, Eagle Claw, and
Pincho were to share the command center in the middle.
Eagle Claw hadn't arrived yet and Huber harbored doubts
whether he would.

Huber winced as Jessie yanked out what must've been
the fiftieth cactus needle with some tweezers. Scott,
Hannah, and Alejandro let out a collective "Ohhhh" as
each one was removed. The spine Jessie had just removed
was so long that they all covered their mouths and insisted

to see it up close. Whatever pain he'd experienced when the needles had punctured his skin didn't compare to the pain of having them extracted.

"How did this happen again?" Jessie asked in amusement.

"I told you, we were outrunning the cops and a prairie dog jumped out in front of me. I didn't want to run it over, so I tried to dodge it, then I tripped and fell down the hill into a cactus."

Scott laughed. "I didn't see any prairie dog."

"Can't say I did either," Hannah concurred.

"I'm glad you all think this is funny," Huber griped. "We probably would've been just fine if Scott hadn't been such a genius and brought up the ticket to the highway patrol. *Ouch*!!" He yelped as Jessie pulled out another needle.

"Can I have a turn?" Hannah asked excitedly.

"Sure," Jessie replied and handed her the tweezers. "There are so many that my hand is getting tired. Don't worry, Huber"—she patted his shoulder, causing him to flinch—"we're halfway there."

At her comment, Scott dropped to his knees, took Huber's hand, and burst into song. "Take my hand and we'll make it I swear. Whoa oh . . ."

"Quiet." Huber elbowed him in the chest, putting a stop to any further singing.

Despite Huber's annoyance, it was nice to be safely

back together again with everyone. The lighthearted atmosphere helped distract him from the fact that his parents were still being held captive and that when it came to outwitting and outracing the Brotherhood and Salazar, the odds were stacked against them.

Suddenly the door to the room burst open. Pincho and Carlos entered and shut the door quickly behind them. Carlos, attempting to appear regal and in charge, had finely trimmed his wavy white hair and goatee. He still had a small oxygen tank attached to his hip and a tube running to his nose, but he also had a noticeable spring in his step. Huber thought Carlos carried a militaristic air about him and looked ten years younger since Huber had seen him last. In all likelihood, this would probably be the last adventure of Carlos's life, and it appeared he was going to make the most of it.

"My friends!" Carlos beamed. "I am so glad to see you've made it safely to the Land of Enchantment! Our noble quest continues!" He then turned somber and shook his head. "Pincho told me of your encounter in Colorado with Matón. I'm sure Eagle Claw is in good health and will rejoin our company shortly. Young knight," he said, pointing to Huber, "are you wounded?"

"*Sí, abuelo*," Alejandro said. "*Batalla con un cactus.*"

Huber knew enough Spanish to know what Alejandro said. Everyone erupted in laughter except Carlos, who nodded solemnly.

Pincho's face went beet red and tears silently streamed down his plump cheeks. Once he caught his breath, the laughter made its way out. "It appears he got the better of you this time around. Maybe next time you should just walk away!" He chuckled and took a pull from a huge bottle of Pepto Bismol.

Huber recalled his first meeting with Pincho at a tavern in Spain. All appearances had indicated he was a washed-up con man. However, the man had proved loyal and faithful to his friend Carlos and helped the group escape the Brotherhood's clutches. During the journey overseas, Carlos had demanded that Pincho quit drinking as they began their new quest. Pincho had reluctantly agreed but insisted he needed some kind of bottle in his hand to replace the habit. Apparently, he had developed quite a taste for the pink stuff. Plus, he said it helped with his indigestion.

"Can we just forget about the cactus, please?" Huber asked as Hannah pulled out another needle. "What's the plan here?"

"Yes." Carlos pointed his finger in the air. "We must stay focused on the task at hand. Before you arrived, we were able to locate Malia's family. They live on the Mescalero Reservation, almost two hours from here. Pincho and a handful of us will head out first thing in the morning and inform them of the events that transpired in Salamanca. From there, we will set out to find the girl and my nephew, Juan Hernán." He shook his head in disappointment.

Huber could see the sadness in the man's face. His own nephew had tried to kill him and deceive him on multiple occasions. After all Carlos had done for Juan Hernán—rescuing him from a troubled household—he still held out hope that his nephew would eschew his evil ways. Huber held no such feelings about the man. He had seen his soul up close and believed the man to be rotten to the core. Huber could scarcely believe the two men were actually related.

Carlos continued, "After securing Malia, we will press on to find and destroy the Golden Staff of Cíbola."

"Any idea how we're gonna do all that?" Scott asked.

Carlos's eyes took over a glazed look as he peered heavenward. "A pathway will always present itself to those upon a righteous quest. Do not doubt, young ones. Our faith will be tested, our resolve pushed to the limit, but we shall prevail." He balled his fist.

Huber looked over at Jessie. "I see the trip hasn't dampened his enthusiasm."

She smiled and shook her head. "No, if anything he is more encouraged then ever."

"After you've finished dressing Master Hill's wounds, please retire to your assigned room. We have a long and, I fear, dangerous adventure ahead of us."

Before exiting the room, Carlos turned and put his

finger in the air as if he'd had an epiphany. He then pulled something from the bag he had slung around his shoulder. It appeared to be a bottle of cologne or aftershave. He approached Huber, who was still lying on his stomach. "We cannot afford an infection on this journey. Don't worry, brave knight. You'll barely feel a thing."

Huber peered over his shoulder. "What is he—"

Before Huber could finish, Carlos had uncapped a small bottle of aftershave and was drizzling the liquid on Huber's back. The blood-curdling scream must've rattled the other guests at the inn. Within seconds, the phone in the room rang. Hannah answered and insisted to the manager that everything was okay. Her brother had just seen a tiny spider in the bathroom and freaked out.

Early the next morning, Huber's back was considerably better. Maybe the aftershave had done the trick after all. Huber, Jessie, and Pincho had all piled into the van Carlos had rented and were just arriving at the Mescalero Reservation. Everyone had agreed that a smaller contingency would be less intimidating to her family than the whole group showing up. Hannah, Scott, Alejandro, and Carlos had stayed behind at the motel to do more research on Cíbola and wait in case Eagle Claw showed up. There still had been no word from him. Huber hoped he was okay, but as time went on, his worries deepened regarding their friend.

"How did you find Malia's family?" Huber asked Pincho.

Pincho tapped the side of his head and took a swig of Pepto. "This is how! The brain inside this *cabeza* is almost too smart for its own good. There is no puzzle it cannot solve. Perhaps after this adventure, I will become a detective," he said with starry eyes. "Perhaps I can even secure a reality television show as I go around and solve mysteries."

Huber rolled his eyes.

"How did you really find them?" Jessie asked.

"They were listed in the white pages," he said, shrugging. "Still . . . most would not have bothered to even look there!"

About half an hour later, Pincho checked the address written on a napkin and pulled the van to a stop in front of a small rambler on the reservation.

"This is the place," he said. "Who wants to break the news that their daughter was abducted, rescued, but then abducted again?"

Huber and Jessie went silent. Finally Huber spoke up. "I guess I should. I spent the most time with her."

Pincho smiled. "Be my guest."

Huber thought back to his time in Salamanca chained up inside the Brotherhood's dungeon. He had been nabbed outside a tavern by the diminutive and demonic Susurro, the Sandman King. The man had blown a powdery substance into Huber's face, causing him to fall into a deep sleep. When he awoke, he was sitting inside a grimy, dark cell deep below a castle. Inside the dungeon he had met Malia and learned of her plight. She had been abducted by the Brotherhood at the same time the Dead Man's Treasure had been stolen. Their aim was to force her to translate an ancient golden tablet. Written on the tablet were directions to find the golden city of Cíbola. Malia had refused to translate the tablet and had suffered for months. Of course, after they had escaped the castle with the tablet, it had ended up in the hands of Juan Hernán Salazar and he had taken Malia. Huber couldn't help but wonder if she had gone from the frying pan to the fire, recalling his time stuck in the Colorado mountains with Salazar. He wasn't looking forward to this conversation with Malia's parents.

"Pincho, maybe you should stay in the van," Huber suggested. "They'll probably feel less threatened by two kids than two kids and an unshaven adult nursing a bottle of Pepto Bismol."

Pincho seemed a bit relieved. "Not a problem, *amigo mío*. It's about time for my *siesta* anyhow." He chuckled and took a big swig from the oversized pink bottle. Pincho then turned on the radio to some classical piano, took a sleeping mask from his pocket, placed it around his eyes, and reclined the driver's seat. "Let me know when you're ready for me."

The duo approached the front door, and Huber knocked. A middle-aged woman answered the door. Huber immediately noticed that the woman had similar features to Malia. She seemed a bit alarmed looking upon the pair of kids. She glanced over their shoulder at Pincho snoozing in the driver's side of the van and then back at the kids. "Are you selling Girl Scout cookies? You don't look like a Girl Scout," she said, pointing to Huber.

"I'm Huber. This is my friend, Jessie," he said. "She's from Spain. The gentleman in the van is named Pincho. He's our driver. Can we come in?"

"Spanish Girl Scout cookies?" she asked. "Very exotic, but I'm really not interested."

"It's about Malia."

The woman paused and her eyes widened. "I am Sunitha, Malia's mother. Please, come in."

Once inside, they were seated on a sofa together in the small living room. Huber felt a bit light-headed when Jessie's knee grazed his on accident. He wondered if and hoped it wasn't an accident.

The woman pulled up a chair across from the sofa where Huber sat. "You have information regarding my daughter?"

Huber thought back to the horrific ordeal that he had endured at the Brotherhood's castle. He had only been there a couple of days. Malia had been there for months. He shuddered to think what that must have been like.

"It's a bit of a long story. We don't know exactly where she is now, but we know where she is likely headed."

"Tell me where she has gone."

For some reason Huber couldn't explain; there was something off in the way Malia's mother was acting. He would have thought that the girl's mother would have been more animated at hearing news of her missing daughter.

"Cíbola," Jessie piped in. "She's on her way to Cíbola to find El Dorado and his Golden Staff."

The woman's eyes widened even further. "Is that a joke?"

"No, it's true," Huber said, backing up Jessie.

Huber related the tale of their experience together within the Brotherhood's castle, sparing no detail regarding the experience he and Malia had endured together. He told Sunitha of meeting her daughter in the grimy cell and the games they were forced to play by the Three Kings, which nearly resulted in their deaths. Huber told the woman how the Brotherhood had obtained a golden tablet that they had tried to force Malia to translate. Their aim was to find their way to the ultimate prize— El Dorado and his Golden Staff. They would wield it as a weapon of sorts to restore the Spanish empire of Coronado's day and rule the world as its three kings: Susurro, Matón, and Fausto. Huber described the acts of Halcón, a masked hero who had engineered their escape, only to betray them in the end, taking Malia and the tablet for himself. Their masked hero had turned out to be Juan Hernán Salazar, and they could only assume that Salazar had taken Malia and somehow succeeded where the Brotherhood had failed in forcing her to translate the tablet. But Huber and his friends were determined to find Malia and stop Salazar and the Brotherhood.

Malia's mother looked at them all gravely. They waited for her to say something. Finally, she did. "I know."

"What do you mean, you know?" Huber asked, taken aback.

"My name is Sunitha. It is a name passed down through the generations within my family line. My ancestor, who bore the same namesake, escaped the clutches of Francisco Coronado, aided by a kind priest named Marcos de Niza. Coronado and his men conquered her village and stole this golden tablet of which you speak. Sunitha was among a select few who had been taught the language of Cíbola and was capable of translating the tablet. The tablet was stolen from her village by Coronado and his men, but it was useless because they could not read it. Sunitha went into hiding, and fortunately his men never found her. She passed on the knowledge of the Cíbolan language to her daughter, and she to her daughter, and so on down to me."

Jessie spoke up. "So you've been teaching the language to Malia as well?"

The woman nodded. "Yes, but her knowledge is

incomplete. I imagine she would be able to translate por-
tions of the tablet, but not all."

Suddenly, a figure appeared from the hallway. Huber
jumped to his feet. Juan Hernán Salazar was smiling
broadly. His appearance was ragged and unkempt, his
clothes dusty. He sported a wispy beard of several weeks
growth, which partially concealed the long scar that ran
down the left side of his face. In his hands, he held El
Dorado's golden tablet.

"Which is why I had to come here to obtain the full
translation," he said. "I've been wandering this barren
countryside long enough."

Jessie was instantly on her feet as well, ready to rush.

"He arrived just before you did," Sunitha said sadly.
"I'm sorry. He threatened my daughter's life if I let on."

"Sunitha, please ask your guests to sit back down."
Salazar looked upon the two in a conniving fashion. "A
bit of a reunion, isn't it, Yoo-ber? Our fates are inter-
twined, it seems."

"Juan Hernán," Huber said with disdain. "Where's
Malia?"

Salazar ignored his comment but burned a hole
through him with his bluish-white eye, which had been
blinded through injury. No matter how many times
Huber saw the man's scarred eye, he shuddered, recalling
his many nightmares.

"Yoo-ber," he said, shaking his head. "You regained

the Dead Man's Treasure, and I allowed you all to go home. You should have followed my advice to stay put with your family."

"We have no family to go home to," Huber responded. "The Brotherhood has abducted our parents."

"They want the same thing as you," Jessie said. "They are probably in New Mexico already."

"Well . . ." Salazar stroked his straggly beard. "They don't have the tablet, do they? Now, everyone, *sit*."

Sunitha motioned for everyone to sit. Reluctantly, they complied.

"What have you done with Malia?" Huber repeated.

"She's safe." He grinned. "With my friend Jack." Salazar pulled out a disposable cell phone. "He is awaiting my call. As soon as he receives it, the girl will be freed and allowed to return here with her family. All I need is the full translation of the tablet."

"How do I know my daughter is safe?" Sunitha asked.

Salazar dialed a number on the phone. Huber could hear the other side ring. Someone picked up.

"Jack, it's me. Put the Zuni girl on." He then handed Sunitha the phone.

Huber watched the woman's face melt with relief as she heard her daughter's voice. Tears streamed as she asked her to hold on. She would soon be safe. Salazar then yanked the phone away from her and hung up.

"The translation now, if you please."

Sunitha took the golden tablet in her hands and exhaled. Salazar retrieved a recorder from his jacket pocket and pushed the record button.

"Here is how the tablet reads: *Be it known that any who seek what lies within the heart of Cíbola will come to ruin. Listen to my tale and do not follow in my footsteps.*

"For many years, I lived in peace within my village. However, I wished to rise above my fellow man and be exalted. One day Uhepono, the god of the underworld, disguised himself as a traveler and bestowed a gift upon me: a Golden Staff topped with an amber stone. Uhepono told me that anything I touched with this stone would be turned to gold. I took the staff and found Uhepono's words to be true. Anything I touched turned to solid gold before my eyes. The people worshipped me as a god and called me the Golden One."

"*Sí,*" Salazar hissed. "The story of El Dorado. I've heard it many times before. Keep going."

"I transformed my humble village of Cíbola into a shimmering golden city. Some of the people desired my gift for themselves. Others feared me and my new power. Many tried to kill me. Others cursed my name and sought rebellion. To avenge these wrongs, I went through the city in the night and touched every sleeping being with my staff, turning them to gold where they lay. Soon thereafter, Uhepono returned in his true form. Miserable, defeated, and alone, I begged Uhepono to take the staff from me. The god of the Underworld refused

and continues to relish in my misery, inhaling my despair as it were sustenance.

"I can no longer endure his presence nor my own. I, Lonan, the once lowly villager, write my own story and solidify my words in gold upon this parchment with my Golden Staff. These are my final words before I turn the stone on myself.

"I will guard the Golden Staff eternally within the clutches of my hands, deep inside the heart of my fallen city, Cíbola. To enter my domain, you must possess the keys of knowledge and answer correctly the riddles of my seven golden sentinels. Only then will you possess this cursed stone and staff. I bid you farewell, and should you find my golden vestige, remove the staff from my hands at your own peril. To find the city of Cíbola, you must . . ."

"Sí, sí, translate the portion your daughter could not." Salazar was almost salivating.

"From Hawikuh, travel south by foot for fifteen days until desert gives way to the mouth of the Rock Monster. Enter the Rock Monster's mouth. By way of flame, follow the symbols leading to my city. Beware of earth, water, black wind, and the face of death. All will impede your way. Once inside the city, you must gain keys from the seven sentinels. Each will progressively test your worthiness. I, Lonan, await your arrival."

"Hawikuh?" Salazar stroked his thin beard. "What does this mean?"

"An ancient pueblo of my people," Sunitha explained.

"It was a humble village. All that is left are the foundations of buildings, ruins."

"Fifteen days south? Rock Monster? Sentinels? Tell me what this means!"

"I held up my end of the bargain. I have no more idea what it means than you. I translated the tablet. Now release my daughter."

Salazar's face took on a look of contempt. Huber had seen it before and feared what evil machinations were running through the man's mind. He redialed the number on the phone.

"Jack, kill the girl."

"No!" Sunitha screamed.

Huber and the others jumped to their feet.

"Then tell me what these things mean!"

Sunitha's eyes brimmed with tears. "Okay," she eeked out. "Just don't hurt her, please."

Salazar returned his attention to the phone. "Hold on, Jack. Don't do anything just yet." He held the phone in his left hand, still connected.

Sunitha took a deep breath. "Fifteen days south is probably around three hundred miles if you think about it. A person can roughly walk about twenty miles a day through this terrain."

Salazar nodded. "Go on."

"The Rock Monster. I honestly do not know what this means. Please believe me! I do know that the terrain to the south turns more rocky. Perhaps he is making reference to a rock formation of some kind."

"And the sentinels?"

"It was rumored in the folk stories passed down to me that Lonan, or El Dorado as you call him, set up a series of traps and obstacles to prevent anyone from reaching him or the staff. These sentinels guard the keys needed to unlock his chamber and collect the staff. This is all I know. Please release Malia."

Salazar's face was unreadable. Finally he brought the phone to his mouth. "Jack, let the girl go."

"Where is she?" her mother implored.

"Close," Salazar said.

A few seconds later, Jack appeared outside the door with Malia. Huber stole a glance behind them to see Pincho gagged and bound in the driver's seat of the van, struggling to free himself.

"They were right outside the whole time?" Jessie said, unbelieving.

Jack popped the screen door open. Huber recognized him instantly. This was the same man Salazar had hired to shadow him on his trip to Salamanca, Spain. He had pretended to be a hippie college-aged student named Willow. His hair was still long and ratty. He had played the part of a hipster so well that Huber never suspected a thing. Only at the end of his journey in Spain did the man show up in a boat to speed Salazar and Malia away, revealing his true identity to Huber and disclosing that his name was actually Jack. "Did you get what you needed, boss?"

"A start."

Jack looked at Huber. "Hey, Huber, man. How's it going? It's me, Willow!" He laughed.

"Whatever he promised you, he'll betray you in the end," Huber responded.

Jack seemed unfazed. "Don't worry about me, little dude. I can take care of myself."

"Yeah, we'll see."

Salazar walked behind Jack and Malia. "Well, it was very good to see all of you again. I sincerely hope this is the last time. I let you live in Spain, and now I will let you go. However, I warn you, if I see any of you again on my journey to Cíbola, I guarantee it will be the last time we meet. Jack, let's go," he barked as if the young man were a dog.

The two men backed out the front door, and Huber and the others bolted outside after them. The men ran to a parked SUV hidden at the side of the house and drove off. Huber noticed the tires on their van had been slashed. Pincho, it seemed, had given up the struggle and just helplessly watched events unfold. Jack must have done it while they were inside. They went back into the house, where Malia and her mother were locked in an embrace. Huber and Jessie let them have a moment. When their reunion was complete, Huber broke the silence.

"Did he hurt you? Where did he take you?"

It appeared that Malia was still in shock at finally being home.

"No, he didn't hurt me. I'm not sure of all of the places we traveled. I was blindfolded most of the time. I did overhear Salazar and Jack talk of what they would do with their treasure. They truly believe they will find Cíbola. I am just so happy to be home at last." Malia looked at her mother. "Where is the rest of the family?"

Sunitha smirked. "Where they've all been for the past several months every morning. Searching the countryside for you. We all feared the worst but couldn't give up looking for you."

"Mother, why did you give him the translation of the tablet?"

Sunitha shook her head. "I had no choice. I couldn't risk losing you again."

"What if he actually finds the Golden City? Can you imagine what will happen if that man ends up with the Golden Staff of Cíbola?"

The woman shook her head and let slip a sly grin. "He won't."

"How do you know that?"

"He will be searching for a long while with the vague directions from that tablet. There is a much faster route to find the city."

Huber straightened up, intrigued. Apparently, the woman had been holding out on Salazar after all.

Sunitha continued. "As you heard earlier, my great ancestor, also named Sunitha, escaped the clutches of Coronado through the assistance of a kind priest. Before she escaped, this same priest, Marcos de Niza, entrusted her with his personal diary, detailing the journey to Cíbola. Whoever possessed this diary would not need the tablet. The diary would lead him straight to the city without the need to decipher the riddles I just read."

"So what happened to it?" Huber asked.

Sunitha pointed to the hardwood floor where Huber stood. She smiled. "It's beneath his feet."

● ● ●

Huber pulled up the loose floorboard beneath the spot where he had been standing, revealing a crawl space three feet deep. As the dust bunnies settled, Huber made out a small lockbox resting on the ground. He dropped to his belly, reached inside, and brought out the lockbox, which was about the size of an ordinary shoebox. It was surprisingly heavy and had a combination dial on its face.

Huber handed the lockbox to Sunitha, who spun the dial to four numbers he couldn't see. The top of the box popped open. Lying inside was a leather journal, about five by seven inches, similar in size to a small book. The leather was faded and cracked, but still held together, though its pages were yellowed with age. Sunitha handed the book to Huber.

"This is Niza's journal. It is considered a sacred gift to our family. I am going to loan it to you. Please take care of it. I cannot advise anyone to search for the city of Cíbola. To do so is to court death. However, as it seems you are determined to do so, find Cíbola before that madman does and certainly before Coronado's descendents come for it. With this journal, you will beat them to it. Be especially sure to follow his advice when it comes to the sentinels and avoiding the death traps. Many of his company died searching for El Dorado to give him the knowledge within those pages, or so I've read."

"You've read it, but never actually looked for the city?" Huber said incredulously.

Sunitha shook her head. "I didn't want to start such an obsession. I never entertained the temptation to acquire the Golden Staff. However, now I see someone must find it to protect, or better yet, destroy the power it contains."

"I'll go with them," Malia said.

"No, you certainly will not," her mother replied sternly. "I and your family have been too long without you." Turning to Huber, she said, "We will do what we can from here to support you on your journey, but if you intend to find the city and enter El Dorado's chamber, you will do so alone."

Huber nodded. "I understand. Malia, you've been through enough. Stay here with your family."

The girl shook her head, but the look from her mother put a stop to her protests.

Huber cracked the diary open and noticed how brittle the pages were. The ink was brown, discolored by time. The writing was in Spanish, and though he was becoming more fluent, he wasn't yet to the point where he could read the language very well. He handed the book to Jessie.

"Let's start at the first page."

Jessie turned to the title page and started to translate.

"The handwriting is very difficult to read," she said, squinting. "I will do my best."

"It's okay."

"Here is what it says: *The Story of the Discovery of the City of Cíbola. In obedience to the Most Illustrious Sir Don Antonio de Mendoza, I, Fray Marcos de Niza, member of the Order of St. Francis, set upon this journey on Friday, March 7, 1539.*"

Jessie turned to the next page and slowly read the first entry aloud.

> *March 10, 1539*
>
> *Our party consists of Esteban de Dorantes, a Moor from Africa, and many Indians from the area who tell me of the story of Cíbola and its fallen king, Lonan. They tell me this man turned the city, its residents, and himself to solid gold. A strange story to be*

sure. One I find hard to believe. However, the Indians are adamant that it is true. Some of them say they've seen the city with their own eyes. Today, we arrived to Petatean, a small Indian village. The people fed me well and called me "Sayota," which means man from heaven. I felt welcome and at home, though some made no attempt to hide their contempt for me. My friend Esteban and I must have appeared strange to them.

While sitting around the fire tonight, some of the men once again told me of Cíbola and the golden king, whom I have taken to calling El Dorado, the Golden One. One of the men took something out of his pocket and handed it to me. It was an arrowhead made of gold. He claims this piece came from the city and was passed to him by his father. It was now mine to keep. When I asked if he could take me to the city, he refused, telling me it is cursed and any who seek it will only find death. I assured him my soul was saved and I did not fear death. He again refused, but mentioned there may be some in a village called Vacapa a few days journey from here who would be willing to take us.

Tuesday, March 28
We arrived at Vacapa today. As we were advised, there are several men here willing to take us to Cíbola, though I am still skeptical of their story. While walking upon a rock-laden path, I injured my leg and asked

Esteban to travel with these men the rest of the way to the city. If he found anything of value, I asked him to send back a cross the size of his hand. If he found nothing significant, to send a cross the size of his thumb. He agreed to go and follow my directives.

Friday, April 7
One of the Indians came bearing a cross today the size of a man. This is the signal from Esteban. He has found the golden city of Cíbola! The size of the cross must mean the stories we have been told are true. The man told me that Esteban had indeed discovered the city with the help of a group of friendly Natives called Zuni. These Zuni are supposedly descended from the same tribe as the Cíbolans. They told me he was inside the city, awaiting my arrival. I immediately forgot my injury and asked the man to take me to Esteban.

Wednesday, April 12
I arrived to the entrance of Cíbola today, a gaping hole in the earth called the mouth of the Rock Monster. The local Zuni warned me to stay away from it or perish. I am persisting onward. They say Esteban has already gone deep inside. It never occurred to me that such a grand city could be beneath the earth.

"Wait!" Huber resounded. "The city is underground?"

The thought had also never occurred to him that Cíbola existed below the earth's surface.

"What do you think it means, this Rock Monster?" Jessie asked.

"It must be the entrance to the underground. A massive cave or something," Huber said. He turned to Sunitha. "Are there any huge cave entrances like that a couple hundred miles south of here? I can't imagine something like that would go unnoticed."

"Unless it's not there anymore. Perhaps someone has filled in the entrance," Jessie said.

Sunitha stirred. "There is one place I can think of. Though I can hardly believe it. It is a mammoth system of underground tunnels and caverns in the Guadalupe Mountains. It's called—"

"Carlsbad Caverns!" Huber said excitedly, recalling his story he'd told to the police officer.

Sunitha nodded. "Yes, there is a big entrance to the cave carved into a mountainside of rock. Wait a minute. I have a postcard." The woman rifled through a drawer next to the sofa and pulled out a tattered postcard that read *Greetings from Carlsbad Caverns*. She handed the postcard to Huber. Jessie came to Huber's shoulder to have a peek. The entrance to the park certainly appeared similar to a giant monster mouth carved into the mountainside.

"The mouth of the Rock Monster!" Jessie said. "That has to be it."

Huber doubted himself upon further thought. "Carlsbad Caverns is a national park. Wouldn't someone have come across the city by now if it were in there? It doesn't make sense."

Malia piped in. "We've visited the caverns many times over the years. I remember one of the rangers telling me on a tour that there are possibly hundreds of undiscovered chambers and caves beyond what's been uncovered."

"Maybe Niza's diary can lead us there," Jessie suggested.

Huber nodded excitedly. "Maybe so. Let's head back to the command center and bring the others up to speed."

It was then he remembered Pincho sitting in the van. He looked outside the door at the fuming man, still bound and struggling to free himself in the disabled vehicle.

Huber turned to Sunitha. "You said you could help us out. Any chance we can borrow a car?"

HANNAH WAS GETTING NERVOUS. Huber, Jessie, and Pincho had been gone much longer than they should have been. Scott and Alejandro were bickering as usual, this time about the existence of UFOs. To pass the time earlier in the day, they'd all visited the Roswell UFO museum. Apparently, in July 1947, something had occurred just outside of Roswell. Some said it was a weather balloon struck by lightning, but others believed a flying saucer had crashed; authorities had recovered its remnants, including the passengers—little green men with oval black eyes. At the museum, they'd all marveled at the story, photos, and video re-creations of the event. The alien autopsy struck Hannah the most. Alejandro was convinced the video was real. Scott laughed through the whole thing.

They'd ventured back to the motel to read a few more stories about Cíbola and Coronado, but they hadn't learned anything new or useful. The stories were all vague and incomplete. Carlos was in the room next to theirs. Last Hannah had seen him, he was reading something and mumbling to himself, half asleep.

"I guarantee the alien in that video was all made of rubber! The guts were spaghetti and corn syrup. So fake!" Scott insisted.

"No, Cowboy! I have seen UFOs with my own eyes above the skies of Salamanca. They are real!"

"Yeah, Rico and I saw the Easter Bunny playin' poker with the Tooth Fairy one night at my grandma's kitchen table," Scott said. Back in Spain, Scott had taken to calling Alejandro "Rico" since Alejandro insisted on calling Scott "Cowboy." While at first the nicknames had been thrown at each other in derision, they had since become terms of endearment. "Next thing you're gonna tell me is that they abducted ya and took ya to their mother ship. Of course, I'm sure they wiped your memory so you couldn't remember it!"

"Mother ship?"

"Don't think too hard about it. You might hurt yourself."

Hannah had been listening to this nonsense all day. "Can you two stop for five minutes? You're giving me a headache."

"I'm gettin' one too." Scott rubbed his forehead. "When is that pizza gonna be here? Isn't it supposed ta be free after twenty minutes? Rico, you sure ya gave 'em the right room number?"

Alejandro threw a pair of dirty socks at Scott's head, narrowly missing.

Hannah's phone vibrated in her pocket. She snagged it and saw it was Huber.

"Quiet, it's my brother!"

She picked up the phone and listened intently as Huber related what had just transpired at Malia's home. She gasped as he related the details of Salazar and the tablet, then smiled in triumph as he told her of Niza's journal. He had a good idea where the entrance to the city was and would tell her when he arrived. They would beat Salazar and the Brotherhood to the golden city. They would arrive back to the motel soon.

Hannah hung up the phone and related the information to the others, who shared in the excitement at the good news. Suddenly there was a knock at the door.

"Pizza's here!" Scott shouted. "Forget about Cíbola! Let's eat!"

Hannah bolted to the door and flung it open.

It took a moment for her mind to register what she was seeing. Three men in fine Italian suits, their faces masked in metal. The Three Kings of the Brotherhood! Fausto, Matón, and Susurro.

"Hello, Hannah. Good to see you again," Fausto said and shot his way into the room before Hannah could close the door. The gentle grin etched in his silver mask and the chain mail beard that hung below betrayed his true demeanor.

Memories of Salamanca flooded Hannah's mind, and her body went slack. Hannah had never guessed that Fausto was actually pretending to be a run-of-the-mill junior high Spanish teacher. She had known the man for over a year. When they traveled to Spain, he had come with them as their chaperone and duped everyone when he pretended to be abducted by the Brotherhood. It was his abduction that had further fueled Hannah, Huber, and the others' desire to find the Brotherhood's headquarters.

It was revealed within the Brotherhood's throne room of their Segovia castle that Mr. Mendoza was in reality Fausto, leader of the Brotherhood. He had been living in disguise, pretending to teach at Carbondale Junior High while secretly searching for the Dead Man's Treasure. When the treasure was discovered by Huber, Hannah, and Scott, he had been watching the whole thing undetected. Huber, Hannah, and Scott had left the treasure in its place, deciding it was morally right to leave it alone. Hannah recalled the sick feeling she had felt when they'd found out the treasure had been stolen just a short time later. They had no idea it was Mr. Mendoza, or rather Fausto, behind the theft.

"Scott, call the cops!" Hannah shrieked.

Susurro giggled and held up a small, thumb-sized device that made a high-pitched whining sound when he pushed a button. The lights in the room flickered and then came back on. "Go ahead and try."

Scott pulled out his cell. It was completely dead. Hannah pulled out her phone. Same story.

"A mini EMP. The technological wonders money can buy these days. All of your phones are dead," Fausto said.

Alejandro dove for the room phone connected to the landline, but Matón beat him to it and ripped the cord from the wall, growling in pleasure.

Carlos came crashing in from the adjacent room, roused from his slumber.

"What's happening here?" he boomed. Upon seeing the Three Kings, he stopped abruptly. "Ahh, *El Rey Fausto*, I see you have come back for another besting?"

The words must have hit a sore spot. Back in Spain, the old man had defeated Fausto in a fencing match to win Huber and Malia's freedom. Fausto slowly and deliberately stepped toward the old man until they were face-to-face.

"You mistake courage for foolhardiness, wisdom for ignorance, and bravery for nitwittedness. You are an old, pathetic man. Do you truly believe you are capable of stopping us? Do you realize you've led these young children into danger and in all likelihood death by taking them on this *noble* quest?"

Carlos's face fell at his words.

Fausto, noticing his expression, pressed on. "How do you think this will end, *viejo*? An old man with a ragtag group of kids against the Brotherhood of Coronado?"

"Where's Eagle Claw?" Hannah yelled, looking at Matón.

The giant's shoulders convulsed in deep laughter. "Put up a good fight, that one, but not good enough."

Hannah's stomach sank. "What did you do to him?"

Matón kept chuckling but said nothing more.

Fausto turned his attention back to the old man. "We've been watching you since you arrived. Imagine our disappointment when we realized you didn't have the tablet that you stole from us in *España*. Not to worry—we'll find Salazar in due time and he'll get what's coming to him. Now," Fausto said, turning toward Hannah, "imagine our pleasure and surprise upon overhearing a phone conversation that the journal of Fray Marcos de Niza has not only been discovered, but is also on its way here into our hands. We will no longer need the tablet."

Hannah's mouth dropped open. "How did you—"

Susurro held up another small device. "Again, amazing the things money can buy."

The Brotherhood must have used the device to eavesdrop on their conversation.

"I'll scream!" Hannah threatened. "People will hear!"

"Go ahead." Fausto flicked his arm upward. As he did, a dagger flew from his sleeve into his outstretched fingers. He held it to Carlos's neck. "*Viejo* here will pay the price if you do."

"*Abuelo!*" Alejandro lunged toward his grandfather.

Before he could reach him, Matón had Alejandro wrapped up and tightly restrained. Susurro slinked toward the boy and blew some kind of powder into his face. Seconds later, Alejandro was unconscious and on the floor.

"Anyone care to join him?" Fausto pointed to Alejandro twitching on the ground.

Suddenly, the door to the room flew open. Huber, Jessie, and Pincho entered. The sight of the Three Kings took them by surprise. Huber obviously hadn't expected to see his former captors.

"Huber," Fausto said happily. "Glad you could join us. If you would, please hand over Niza's diary. You have my promise that if you do so peacefully, we'll leave without any further incident.

Huber's brows furrowed in surprise, and he tried to act dumb. "Diary? What are you—"

"They listened in on our conversation," Hannah interrupted. "They know you have Niza's diary that leads to Cíbola."

"Young knight!" Carlos shouted. "Do not listen to

the vain promises of this grand enchanter! His words are venom and lies. Take the guide to Cíbola and run!"

Pincho disagreed with his friend. "Huber, give him the diary. It's not worth anyone's life."

Jessie backed up the sentiment. "Do it, Huber. Don't let anything happen to *Abuelo*."

Hannah watched as Huber reluctantly stepped forward with the cracked, brown book. Fausto continued to hold the blade to Carlos's throat. Hannah imagined the disappointment of Sunitha and Malia after finding out they lost the diary after possessing it for only a couple of hours.

"Hand the diary to Matón," Fausto whispered to Huber.

Hannah looked up at the gruesome face of Matón the King Crusher and sighed as her brother placed the book in the brute's hand.

"I bet beneath that mask, Eagle Claw bruised you up good." Huber's voice quivered just a tad.

Matón growled and balled his fist but restrained himself.

Hannah turned her gaze to Fausto and spoke. "You got what we wanted. Now hold up your end of the deal."

"Susurro, Matón," Fausto said. "Let's leave them in peace."

Hannah watched in confusion as the three men sharply inhaled. Without warning, Susurro threw a glass vial with clear liquid against the wall. The room was instantly filled with some kind of vapor that burned Hannah's eyes. She inhaled a small amount of the thick gas. A drowsy sensation began to trickle from her head down to her toes. She remembered her brother relating how Susurro had blown some kind of substance into his lungs in Spain, causing him to pass out and experience terrible nightmares. Hannah shook with fear, wondering what kind of dreams awaited, compliments of *El Rey Susurro*, the Sandman King. She looked around and saw the others droop and slump toward the ground as she did. She made eye contact with Huber just before her lids closed, and she hit the floor.

● ● ●

Huber was running, hopelessly lost within a cavernous maze of stalactites and limestone walls. His heart pounded, and deep down he knew he'd never find his way out. Within the corridors of rock, unnatural sounds wafted his way—shrieks of terror, booms, and growls. They came from all directions. Something was closing in on him—the darkness. He saw it billowing toward him like a massive rolling cloud. His flashlight could not penetrate its depth. He did an about-face to run the way he'd come, but it was no use. A separate plume of darkness was spilling its way from that direction as well. To his left on the path where he was standing, he noticed a small pool of water. Having no other escape route, he jumped into the water. The temperature was freezing, and it felt like some kind of awful force was sucking him under. He waved his arms, not knowing which way he was swimming. He was drowning!

Suddenly, the current changed and propelled him upward toward a tiny shaft of light. Just as he was about to inhale the frigid water, his head broke through the surface. He pulled himself out of the water and onto a rocky, narrow ledge that merged with a bridge over the water. He was in a massive dome-shaped cavern. From somewhere up above, a shaft of sunlight was beaming down on a tiny circular island where the path led. Shivering, Huber walked toward the island, hoping the light would warm and dry him.

As he drew nearer, he noticed the light reflecting off certain objects, statues of some kind. For some reason, an unsettling feeling crawled up from his gut. He kept going forward and finally reached the island. As he gazed upon the statues placed in a circle, a scream tried to fight its way out, but it stayed lodged deep inside. He stood frozen. The statues were not statues; they were people, and not just anyone. Hannah, Scott, Jessie, Alejandro, Pincho, Carlos, and his parents were all standing around the perimeter of the island, their faces frozen in terror, their bodies solidified in gold. Huber touched his sister's face. It was cold and hard. Suddenly, her eyes moved and met his. Startled,

Huber fell backward into the light and looked down at his hands as they turned to gold.

Finally, the scream erupted. As it did, he awoke in the motel room with a pounding headache. The gas that Susurro had released had dissipated, and Huber noticed everyone groggily rising to their feet, rubbing their heads. Everyone except for Carlos, who lay still on the floor. His chest was not moving.

"*¡Abuelo, despierta!*" Jessie shook her grandfather.

Alejandro was instantly at her side, joining her. The old man did not stir, and the color was drained from his face.

"Call the medics!" Alejandro cried.

Their cell phones fried, Huber raced to the landline and reconnected the wire into the jack where Matón had ripped it out. He picked up the receiver and heard a dial tone. He dialed 911 and was instantly connected to a dispatcher. Within minutes, an ambulance arrived. The paramedics peeled Alejandro and Jessie away from their grandfather and attempted to resuscitate him. Their attempts seemed to be in vain.

One of the paramedics removed a machine from a bag, a defibrillator. She turned on the machine, opened Carlos's shirt, and placed the two pads over his chest. She gave his heart a shock. Momentarily, his torso lifted off the ground, but he took no breath. She tried again with no luck. The third time his chest lifted off the ground, the old man inhaled and gasped. His eyelids fluttered momentarily, then shut as he coughed wildly. The other medic quickly hooked him back up to oxygen and helped lift him onto a stretcher. They would take him to Lovelace Regional Hospital.

Pincho drove them all to the facility in the SUV they'd borrowed from Sunitha. After waiting for what seemed to be hours within a cramped waiting room, a doctor came out to advise everyone of the old man's condition. Huber believed the look on her face didn't bode well for Jessie and Alejandro.

"How is our *abuelo*?" Jessie asked. "Can we see him?"

The doctor nodded. "Yes, you can see him. Follow me."

Maybe Huber had misread the doctor's face. They followed her into a dim-lit room. It appeared that Carlos was sleeping peacefully. He was hooked into an IV, and a machine kept track of his heartbeat. Huber sighed in relief. It appeared he was okay. Alejandro was instantly at his grandfather's side.

"*Abuelo*, can you hear me?" He rubbed the old man's hand.

The doctor shook her head. "I'm sorry, son. He can't hear you."

"What do you mean?"

"The paramedics brought him back from the brink of death, but we haven't been able to wake him. He's comatose."

"Comatose?" Alejandro asked, confused at the word.

Hannah put her hand on his shoulder. "It means he's nonresponsive, unable to wake up."

"For how long?" Jessie asked.

The doctor shrugged. "Could be hours, days, weeks, or months. There's no way to tell. Luckily, he's well insured so he can stay here as long as it takes. I'll give you all some time," she said and stepped out of the room.

Alejandro backed away from his slumbering grandfather and slumped into a vacant seat.

"Sorry about all this, Rico," Scott attempted to console him. "He didn't deserve this. He was a good guy."

"Do not speak of him in a past tense!" Alejandro almost shouted. "He *is* a good guy and will be okay!"

"Yeah, I know," Scott said quietly. "Sorry, didn't mean it like that."

"What should we do now?" Huber asked. "Carlos is out of commission, Salazar has the tablet, and the Brotherhood has Niza's journal. Not to mention Eagle Claw is still gone."

Jessie spoke up. "*Abuelo* would not want us to give up the search. The Brotherhood still has your parents. We must find them. We know the city is somewhere inside Carlsbad Caverns. That's a start. The Brotherhood doesn't know that. We can beat them there."

"Then what?" Scott asked. "Without a guide, we'd just be wanderin' a bunch of tunnels and caves, gettin' lost. I've done that once already and don't plan on doin' it again. We need the diary."

"No, we don't," Huber said playfully.

"What do ya mean?"

Huber motioned to Jessie, who pulled out what appeared to be sheets of photos.

"We stopped at Kinko's on the way back. We copied each page of the diary just to be safe. The copies are very high resolution. In many ways, it will be better than the actual pages themselves."

"We thought it'd be a good idea to have a backup. Looks like we were right. If we go soon, we can beat the Brotherhood there."

Pincho took a swig of Pepto and interrupted, misty-eyed. "I'm sorry all of you got caught up in this mess. Don Carlos is my best friend. I cannot leave him here."

Huber nodded. "Stay to protect him. Plus it will be nice for him to have a friendly face nearby when he wakes up."

"So we're just supposed to go and take on the Brotherhood by ourselves?" Alejandro asked.

"Not by yourselves," a deep, calm voice startled them from behind.

In unison they turned to see an imposing figure standing in the doorway. Huber couldn't believe his eyes. A bit beat up and sporting a black eye, but otherwise appearing healthy, Eagle Claw stood before them!

CHAPTER
• 5 •

ROLLING DOWN THE HIGHWAY toward Carlsbad
Caverns, the group listened as Eagle Claw retold the story
of how he had escaped Matón and the Brotherhood. They
had brawled for some time. Eagle Claw had locked Matón
in a headlock until he was about to pass out. That was the
moment when Matón's henchmen jumped in to save their
king from losing. Eagle Claw had been hit over the head
with a blunt object and almost passed out, causing him to
lose his grip. The ruckus must have caused the neighbors
to call the police because he had heard sirens screaming
toward the house. At the sound, Matón and his men had
fled, leaving Eagle Claw. He had quickly made his escape
and hitchhiked his way to New Mexico. Evidently, there
weren't too many people willing to pick him up based on
his beat-up appearance, and Huber couldn't blame them.

Huber had never felt so relieved to see anyone in his life. Having a true warrior in their midst had boosted everyone's spirits considerably. Luckily, Sunitha had agreed to let them borrow the family's SUV for the duration of their journey. They'd gone back to the motel and packed up everything that they may need for an underground adventure.

"Before leaving Colorado, I made sure your dog is being looked after by your neighbors," Eagle Claw said.

The statement relieved Huber. "Thanks for taking care of him."

Alejandro and Jessie were busy in the backseat, trying to decipher Niza's handwriting. Huber could only hope that the Brotherhood was still trying to decipher the cryptic directions speaking of vague distances and rock monsters.

"How about a rest?" Eagle Claw asked from the driver's seat. "Anyone hungry?"

Huber had almost forgotten about eating. Now that he thought about it, he was starving, and the Village Inn up ahead sounded fantastic. Everyone nodded their agreement except Scott, who said he'd rather eat roadkill doused in gasoline, but the majority prevailed.

As they sat around the table, Jessie retrieved the images, careful to not spill maple syrup on them.

"Have you been able to translate more entries?" Huber asked with a mouthful of strawberry crepes.

"The most difficult part is making out his handwriting. It gets worse as it goes on, probably because he was writing in the dark, but I believe we have been able to make out the next few days of Niza's journey."

Huber and the others listened intently as Alejandro read:

Thursday, April 13

By the light of my lamp I write these words within this dark underworld. Luckily, I was able to acquire a guide who says he knows the ancient Zuni-Cíbolan language. He claims there are but few who know how to decipher the symbols. However, he and my other guides who had assured me they knew their way through this maze of stone have led us to a standstill. After entering the mouth of the cavern, we encountered thousands of bats. I had never seen such a sight! After passing beneath the bats, there were several pathways to follow. My guides led me to a room they call the giant room. Inside this room are several formations of stalagmites that have a grotesque appearance. From this room we continued on and after many minutes of walking down this pathway, we came to a dead end save for a long, dark pit. I tossed a pebble down the pit and could not hear it land. This startled my company, causing them to believe the pit is bottomless. On one of the walls we passed nearby, we noticed the symbol for Cíbola scratched into the rock, a round disk shape containing the skull of a man with hollow eyes wearing a feathered headdress. My guides tell me this symbol is Lonan or El Dorado, the king who turned himself to gold. My guides assure me the way is nearby, but I fear they have led us astray. One of them is sure that this is the portion of the journey where "earth" will try and stop us.

Occasionally coming up from the pit are strange sounds. My guides tell me these are the sounds of demons guarding the city of Cíbola. The guides are frightened and constantly threaten to run away. I fear no darkness nor any demon. Esteban is down there somewhere. I must find him. He is likely still inside the city. We will press on and find him.

"Okay," Huber said. "So we know where to start. What does the next entry say?"

Jessie shook her head. "We have not got that far yet. It took us this long just to figure out this one entry. We'll keep working on the next one. I hope to complete it by the time we arrive."

"How much further is this place, Carl's Junior Caverns? I could really go for a burger right now. I hate pancakes!" Scott said.

Hannah shook her head at him. "Carls*bad* Caverns is just another hour away, and you better fill up because I don't think you'll find any burgers down there."

Alejandro jumped in. "Come now, Cowboy, try some of Huber's crepes. They're French, fluffy, and full of fruit, so you'd probably like them."

Scott rolled his eyes. "Funny."

Eagle Claw interrupted the banter. "Have any of you thought how we're going to be able to go off on our own to explore?"

Huber shrugged. "I bet they have self-guided tours."

"They do," Hannah said. "I looked up the information online. But they also watch to make sure you stay where you should."

"Sneak in at night?" Scott said as he crunched a piece of bacon.

"What?" Huber asked, thinking through the idea.

"Yeah, we'll scope the place out on the tour or whatever, then sneak in after closin' time. Camp inside for the night. Bet there won't be no one in there with the bats and demons and all."

Huber had to admit the idea had merit. "Sounds good to me."

Eagle Claw smiled. "I like the way this one thinks. I'm glad Carlos and Pincho made sure we were well stocked. It looks like we have everything we need to backpack through the Himalayas and survive for a month."

"Okay," Huber said. "We go on the main tour just to scope the place out while Jessie and Alejandro work on the journal entries. Then we'll hang around outside until the place closes and sneak in."

● ● ●

"If you'll follow me," the ranger said, "we'll descend this pathway into the natural entrance of the caverns."

They had caught the final tour of the day, which lasted about an hour and a half. They were being led by a tall, lanky man in a tan uniform and green hat. His name was Mike. They were snaking down a sloped pathway that led past a huge natural amphitheater and straight into a massive hole in the rocky mountainside. Huber could imagine why its early discoverers had called it the mouth of a rock monster. He had the feeling he was about to be swallowed up into a different world. The tour group was small, comprising of Huber, Scott, Hannah, and a few other tourists. Eagle Claw had stayed above the surface with Alejandro and Jessie to keep watch, just in case the Brotherhood or Salazar showed up.

"There are over thirty miles of mapped caves in this system," Ranger Mike continued. "There are many more tunnels and caverns yet to be mapped."

"When were the caverns discovered?" Hannah asked.

"Well," the Ranger answered pensively. "We've found evidence of Native Americans near the site and even inside, so they were probably among the first."

Huber and Hannah looked at each other knowingly.

"The first settler to discover the place was probably Jim White. He was just a sixteen-year-old cowhand who stumbled upon the place while exploring. He built himself a ladder, made his way down into this very entrance, and discovered a massive bat colony. He then discovered that the tunnels continued on, and he ventured further by himself until his kerosene lantern almost went dry. Luckily, he found his way back out and returned with a friend he called 'Muchacho,' and together they explored the cave for three days, leaving a string behind them so they could find their way back out. Anyways, the boys started mining guano to make some extra money."

"What's guano?" one of the small kids on the tour asked.

"Bat manure," the ranger replied.

Scott interrupted. "Wait a sec! These guys mined poop? And got paid for it?"

The ranger chuckled. "Back in those days it was worth ninety dollars a ton, which was good money. Farmers used it as fertilizer. After a while, people started coming to see the caverns for themselves, having heard the tales. Eventually, the place became a hot spot for tourists, and it was designated a national park in October 1923. Jim White was one of the first rangers of the park. The park service created this trail leading down to the entrance;

otherwise you'd be climbing down a rickety old ladder or lowered in a guano bucket."

"That'd be awesome," Scott mumbled to himself.

The ranger continued leading them downward, and soon they were swallowed up in the mouth of the cave. They had entered another dimension, one full of nature's artistry. They were led past the bat cave. Huber looked up at the thousands of sleeping bats and massive piles of guano that Jim White had mined in years past. Next, they were led through a corridor past a formation called Devil's Spring, which looked like a frozen lava flow jutting up out of a small pond. Next, Ranger Mike led them past Green Lake, a pool of water with an eerie green color. They ventured beyond the Queen's Room and King's Chamber with limestone formations that resembled majestic figures. Glossy stalactites hung from the ceiling like giant icicles. Stalagmites rose upward, attempting to join their stalactite brothers coming from the opposite direction. Where some had met, they had become huge columns, seeming to support the weight of the mammoth cavern. The ranger explained that the stalactites and stalagmites had been formed over many thousands of years. Huber noticed a stalagmite's tip was missing.

"What happened to that one?"

"One of our visitors broke it off," the ranger replied sadly.

A sense of sadness mingled with anger washed over

Huber. He could tell Hannah and even Scott felt the same way. It had taken thousands of years for the stalagmite to grow and only seconds for someone to ruin it. It seemed an insult to nature's patience.

"Want to feel something really unsettling?" Ranger Mike asked.

No one replied.

"I'll take that as a yes. Hold your hand in front of your face."

Everyone did so.

The ranger then flipped a switch on the wall, instantly plunging everyone into darkness. Huber could feel the breath on his hand, but he couldn't see it. He had been in darkness like this once before inside the mine at Dead Man's Treasure, but the darkness inside these caverns seemed almost penetrating. His breath quickened as he fought the panic of being in complete darkness. Just as quickly, the ranger flipped the switch again, illuminating their path.

Next, they entered what was called the Big Room. The size and scope of the room took his breath away. The ranger indicated the room was eight acres in size. Huber drank it in. The lights around the cavern cast unearthly shadows and many colors everywhere. There were benches in the center of the room. The ranger indicated they'd take a break, then continue on. The three went and sat down to rest their feet.

"This has to be the room Niza was talking about," Huber said. "The Giant Room."

"I think you're right." Hannah nodded. "Definitely matches his description."

The ranger called the tour group back together. "One last stop on our tour," he said. "The Bottomless Pit!"

From the Big Room, they trekked past Mirror Lake, another small body of water that was crystal clear and only looked a few inches deep. In reality, the ranger said it was many feet deep. The deception came about because the water was so still.

A short distance from Mirror Lake, they approached a gaping black chasm that was probably twenty feet in length and about the same in width—the Bottomless Pit. The massive hole descended downward into thick blackness. Across the chasm and inaccessible to visitors was a rope ladder, held together by mere threads. Just peering over the edge sent a sense of foreboding coursing through Huber's veins.

"It ain't really bottomless, is it?" Scott asked the ranger.

"Care to find out?" he joked. "Here." He handed Scott a penny from his pocket. "Toss it in."

Scott tossed the penny inside the hole.

"Listen," Ranger Mike said, smiling. "Did you hear it?"

"I didn't hear nothin'."

"Exactly! Normally, you'd hear the coin ricochet off the bottom. If it did, it was so far away, we couldn't hear it."

"Whoa!" Hannah marveled. "How deep is it?"

The Ranger shook his head. "Not sure. There was a rumor a man went down the pit in the early 1900s looking for lost treasure or something."

Huber and Hannah looked at each other wide-eyed but said nothing.

"What happened to him?"

Ranger Mike shrugged. "No one knows. He never came back out. That deteriorated rope ladder across the way was said to be his way down. Of course, it could all just be a rumor that's grown over the years."

"What was his name?" Huber asked. "The man who went down."

Ranger Mike scratched his head. "I believe his name was Joshua . . . Joshua Cain."

Before turning back to the elevators that would take them back to the surface, Huber took one last look at the pit and then turned to Scott. "I have a very bad feeling about that pit."

CHAPTER
• 6 •

HUBER, SCOTT, AND HANNAH rendezvoused with the others a few hundred yards away from the cave entrance. The tent Eagle Claw had set up was safely tucked away in the brush. Inside, Alejandro and Jessie were busy deciphering Niza's journal. Eagle Claw continued to scout the perimeter to make sure they were safe.

Huber related to Jessie and Alejandro the events of the tour and that they'd found their way to the Bottomless Pit that they believed Niza had referenced.

"Were you able to translate the next section of the journal?" Huber asked.

"Yes," Jessie answered. "Looks like we will need to go down into that pit."

Scott frowned. "I was afraid of that."

"What's the matter, Scotty?" Hannah asked.

"Didn't look so bad to me. Afraid to go down the big scary pit?"

"Yeah."

"I'm not so sure about going down that old ladder," Huber said, backing up his friend.

"*Abuelo* packed some rappelling equipment. We should be able to go down without a problem," said Jessie.

"Yeah." Scott rubbed his head. "Just make sure Rico there isn't holdin' the rope," he said.

Alejandro winked. "Do not worry, Cowboy. I'll take good care of you."

"What does the next entry in the diary say?" Huber motioned to Jessie.

Jessie took out her notebook where she had transcribed the contents.

Friday, April 14

Seeing no other way to progress to the site of Cíbola, we descended the pit yesterday evening. I used a rope to climb down as far as I could go. A member of my party was below me on the rope. I watched as he lost his grip and fell into the darkness. The light from my fire could not find him, but I could hear his voice calling for me to let go of the rope, to take a leap of faith. I took a breath and did so. To my surprise, the darkness buoyed me up and led me to an opening in the side of the pit.

"What do you think he means by that?" Huber asked. "The darkness buoyed him up?"

Jessie shrugged and read on.

> *Once the rest of my party reached where I stood, we traveled through the opening, which led us back onto a narrow path. My guides assured me we had passed the first barrier—earth. The next barrier to overcome is water.*

"Do you have the next entry translated?" Huber asked.

"Not yet," Jessie said. "Patience."

"So, any idea on how we're gonna sneak in after closing time?" Scott asked.

"Yes." Eagle Claw entered the tent, startling everyone.

"Ya gotta quit showin' up like that!" Scott complained.

Eagle Claw let slip a slight grin. "We will attend the nightly bat flight program." He tossed a pamphlet to Huber.

"Bat program?" Hannah asked.

"Each night at dusk, the bats collectively depart the cave in a big swarm. We'll go to the show and get as close as we can to the entrance. While everyone is watching the spectacle, we'll make our way in and hide until the lights go off."

Huber's memory instantly flashed back to when Ranger Mike shut off the lights in the Big Room, plunging them into palpable darkness. He hoped Carlos and Pincho had packed some high-powered flashlights.

"We'll then make our way to the pit," Eagle Claw continued. "Can you recall your way there without a guide?" he asked Huber.

Huber nodded sheepishly, semi-confident he could lead them to the Bottomless Pit. Without lights illuminating their pathway throughout the caverns, though, it'd be easier said than done.

"We have one hour until dusk. Continue working on translating the next portion of Niza's journal and we'll pack up with gear and supplies, then make our way down. Everything is in the SUV. Come get outfitted."

● ● ●

Never in Huber's life had he witnessed such a spectacle as he beheld hundreds of thousands of bats swarming overhead in unison like a vortex. The sun was painting a spectacular vista of warm oranges and reds over the Guadalupe Hills, enhancing the atmosphere. A woman ranger with a microphone was describing the seventeen different species of bats, some from as far away as Brazil. They would depart the cave, feast on over one ton of insects in the desert, and return to the cave just before dawn. As the crowd was engrossed in the scene, Eagle Claw motioned for them to follow him inside the cave. It was difficult for Huber to pull himself away from watching the hypnotic flight patterns of the bats as they performed their dance of the night. At last, Jessie pulled him out of his trance, and with great stealth, the six of them slipped inside the cavern entrance undetected. Just inside the corridor, they found a small alcove to hide in just beyond the Witch's Finger, a tall, knotted stalagmite that resembled its namesake. It must have been fifteen feet high.

Huber held his breath as several park rangers walked along the lighted corridor just ahead of them. They were engrossed in conversation and kept walking toward the exit. Huber exhaled, and as he did, the lights illuminating the caverns went out. The darkness was invasive and cold. Huber was instantly back inside the mine at Dead Man's Treasure. His body began to involuntarily shake. To quell his anxiety, he reached out his hand. It was met by a soft, warm hand in return. He knew it was Jessie. He took a deep breath and suddenly a flashlight was in his face.

"Ohhh," Scott swooned. "The lights go out for two seconds and these two can't help themselves."

Huber looked down and noticed his hand was still interlocked with Jessie's. He quickly released his grasp. His face smoldered volcano red.

Eagle Claw changed the subject. "Everyone get out your flashlights. I'm guessing we've got a long way to go." He then turned to Scott. "By the way, when the going gets rough, don't ask me to hold *your* hand."

● ● ●

Though the pathway appeared differently without the lights, Huber and the others were able to guide their group through the rooms they'd traversed earlier in the day. Huber had almost stumbled into Mirror Lake, but Alejandro caught him before he did. They found the Bottomless Pit, and Eagle Claw anchored their rappelling lines in the rock at the top. Rappelling into a deep, dark, bottomless hole was not Huber's ideal way of spending his evening. The words of Ranger Mike regarding Joshua Cain kept finding their way into his thoughts.

Huber couldn't help but think that going down would be the easy part; getting back up would be the challenge. He felt secure as Eagle Claw tied the rope around his waist and assured him it was strong. Why he had volunteered to go down first, he wasn't sure. If it were under different circumstances, the process may have even been fun. Taking a breath, Huber crawled backward over the edge and pushed off. His legs bounced off the wall of the pit as he made his way down. To his surprise, rappelling was easier than he thought. It seemed to come naturally. The light from Huber's spelunker helmet bounced off the sides of the pit. Every member of the team was wearing a similar helmet with a light affixed to the top. As he peered downward, the light penetrated ten feet or so and was then absorbed by darkness. Looking upward, he saw Hannah and Scott following behind him.

"How long is this rope again?" he yelled upward. It seemed the darkness just kept going and going.

"Hundred and twenty feet," someone yelled from the top. Huber thought it was Alejandro.

Huber's concern was that the rope was going to run out of slack before he reached the bottom. He lessened his grip, allowing himself a bit more speed. As he did, he descended faster than he had intended. His feet bounced off the sides of the wall, causing him to lose his balance and let go of the rope. He fell fast and tried to regain his grip. The friction from the rope burned his hand, preventing him from getting a handle.

In free fall, all he could do was yell and pray. The light from his helmet careened everywhere and bounced off the walls, casting demented shadows. He was still attached to his harness by the rope and did his best to slow his fall by dragging his feet against the side of the wall. Suddenly, he hit the end of the rope and momentarily tugged upward, dropped back down, and then stopped altogether. Hannah and Scott yelled from somewhere up above. Their voices were coming closer. A sickening feeling hit Huber as he realized the force of his fall must have jarred everyone else loose on the line. Huber peered upward and made out a body flying toward him. It was Hannah. He braced for impact. Seconds later, she slammed into him like a bullet. The force sent Huber's spelunker helmet flying into the darkness, flipping around and then disappearing.

Immediately afterward, Scott came crashing into the two of them. They all moaned in pain as they dangled and flopped like fish caught in a dip net.

"I think I got whiplash," Scott complained, rubbing his neck.

"I'd take whiplash over being sandwiched between the two of you," Hannah complained. "When is the last time either of you showered?"

"'Bout three days ago," Scott moaned, turning his head toward Huber.

"Scott!" Huber called. "Can you see the bottom?"

Angling his helmet downward, Scott observed the never-ending darkness.

"No, nothin' but pitch black."

Someone yelled from up above, but they were so far away and the echo so intense within the pit, no one could decipher their words.

"What do we do now?" Hannah asked.

"Guess we'll have to climb our way back up and get a longer rope."

"No way!" Huber said. "Just have Eagle Claw pull us—"

Before Huber could finish his sentence, the knot around his harness broke beneath the collective weight. Hannah reached out and grasped her brother's hand, gritting her teeth as Huber's legs dangled above the gaping blackness.

"I can't hold you," she gasped. "Scott, help me!"

"I can't!" he yelled out helplessly. "He's too far away."

Huber looked over his shoulder at the darkness waiting to engulf him and could only imagine how far he would fall before he finally hit bottom. His hand was sweaty and he could tell Hannah was struggling. His hand slipped loose from hers, and he saw her face diminish as he fell downward. It was like a bad dream where he was falling out of control and waking up before he hit the ground. Only this time, Huber was sure he wouldn't wake up. After all, there was no such thing as a bottomless pit.

Before his sister's face disappeared completely, Huber felt his legs hit and sink into something soft. He was no longer falling, but everything around him was still pitch black, as if he were suspended in air. It was then he reached down to touch the darkness and realized it had substance. His hand touched something else that seemed hard and plastic-like. As he lifted it, a light shined from the object. It was his spelunker helmet. The front of the helmet with the light had landed in whatever substance he was standing. He shined the light from the helmet over the ground. He was standing waist deep in fine black sand.

"Huber!" Hannah screamed. "What happened? Are you okay?"

"Sand!" he shouted upward to her barely visible face thirty feet above him. "Black sand!"

The sand had given the illusion that there was no end

to the pit as it camouflaged perfectly with the walls. Huber dug around and found a quarter from 1965, along with many other coins that had been swallowed up over the years. No wonder they hadn't made any noise. Off to his right, he saw an opening in the rock wall about the height and width of a person. Huber remembered the entry from Niza about taking a leap of faith to find the door leading onward. This must've been what he had referenced. Huber shuffled his way to the top of the sand pile and dragged himself to the opening, climbing onto the ledge.

"Jump down!" He stuck his head out and yelled to Hannah.

"Are you crazy?" she shouted in response.

"It'll be fine. The landing is really soft. Just let me get out of the way first."

Huber ducked inside the opening, heard a soft thud, and felt the sand particles fly up around his face. He then pulled Hannah up.

She laughed. "Guess we were lucky your harness came undone."

"I didn't feel so lucky at the time."

Huber shouted for Scott to follow suit, and within a few minutes, everyone else had made the leap of faith into the sandbar.

Crowded into the opening, Huber stole a glance at Jessie and smiled. "So, the earth tried to stop us. What did Niza say is next?"

Jessie pulled out the photocopy of Niza's next entry out of her pack and read:

Friday evening, April 14

The rest of my party having made the leap of faith successfully, we continued onward through the hole in the rock. The passageway was narrow, making it necessary to walk single file. The air was cold here and sometimes difficult to breathe. As we made our way out of the passageway, we came onto a stone bridge within a water-filled cavern. Across the bridge is a golden door etched with the symbol of Cíbola. We are on the right track! A guide related he had once come this far as a child and said one of us must dive deep into the water to find a lever to open the door. After pulling the lever, he assured me we would find our way. I, myself, not being aquatically adept, asked that he make the dive.

"Lovely," Scott said. "Any of you Acapulco cliff divers?"

"No," Jessie answered. "However, I am a good swimmer. My family used to vacation at the Canary Islands. I've jumped off my fair share of cliffs. I can do it."

CHAPTER 7

SHIMMYING HIS WAY THROUGH the narrow crooks and crannies brought upon Huber an extent of claustrophobia he had never experienced. At any second he believed the walls might crash in on him, trapping him in the underground tomb forever. Looking at the faces surrounding him, he gathered similar thoughts were swimming around in their heads. What brought him comfort was that Hannah was just behind him, talking to him in conversation as if they were walking down a wide sidewalk.

"So, it's really a shame you didn't get to see the UFO museum," she said casually.

"Yeah," Huber groaned as he squeezed through a crevice. "Why's that?"

"They had some really interesting displays about the

UFO crash in Roswell. Alejandro believed it was true. Scott said it was a weather balloon and people are just making it all up."

"What do you think?" Huber asked.

"I don't know. I've never seen anything like it before. I don't suppose it's probable, but maybe it's not impossible. I think people want to believe there's some kind of mystery left out there, that we're not all alone in the universe."

"Yeah, you're probably right," Huber said, thinking about their quest. "Maybe it's the same thing with the Golden Staff of Cíbola. Maybe it's all just made-up stories that people want to believe. If it's true that means there's still something supernatural or magical in the world."

Huber looked back at Jessie, who was just behind Hannah, to see her nodding in agreement. "Then I guess we are no different. Look at us down here. I sincerely hope we're not chasing leprechauns."

"Me too," Huber agreed. "If there's no pot of gold at the end of this rainbow, I'll be pretty upset."

"What are y'all yappin' on and on about?" Scott asked from behind Jessie.

"Aliens," Huber replied. "You think they're fake, eh?"

"Of course they are!"

"What about the Golden Staff? Think it's fake too?"

"Of course it ain't!"

Huber smiled at Hannah and Jessie, shrugging his shoulders. Up ahead, Eagle Claw shouted that they were approaching an exit out of the tunnel. Huber quickened his pace and shuffled his way forward until his light revealed Eagle Claw stepping through the crevice. Huber followed suit and stepped out onto a ledge that narrowed into a kind of natural rock bridge. It was broken apart into pieces, like stepping stones. To cross, they'd have to hop their way from one landing to another until they reached the other side. On both sides of the bridge was crystal still water. The moist walls inside this cavern were a splash of colors: green, orange, and yellow. Huber remembered Ranger Mike telling them that the various colors were caused by oxidation. The drop to the water's surface was about ten feet from where they stood.

Soon everyone else crawled their way through the tunnel and out onto the ledge. Huber lifted his head and shined his light toward the other side. What he saw amazed him and affirmed his faith that there actually could exist something magical in the world. Upon the opposite ledge was a door, but not just any door. It was a work of art, composed of solid gold. Upon its face was a carving of a skull staring soullessly ahead at them. Upon his crown was a headdress with long arcing feathers.

"El Dorado," Huber whispered to himself as the others stared ahead in stunned silence at the golden door.

Jessie and Alejandro ripped out the page referencing the door and reread the passage, their hands shaking with excitement.

"We have to dive in the water and find a lever to open that door," she said. "I'll do it. *Abuelo* thought of everything. There is a wet suit in one of the packs. I'll go back inside the tunnel and change."

The wet suit was in Hannah's pack. Jessie scurried back into the tunnel and a few minutes later reentered the cavern, appearing as if she were ready to go surfing. Eagle Claw asked if she was sure about the dive. She nodded, and he wrapped a rope around her waist so he could pull her back up to the ledge if there was any trouble.

"Okay, wish me luck!"

"Wait!" Huber said. "Remember that the water is deeper than it looks."

"Okay." She smiled and crouched down, ready to dive.

"Hold on!" he said again.

She sighed and stood back up. "What now?"

"Look carefully where you jump. You wouldn't want to dive onto a stalagmite or something."

"I'll be careful." She shook her head and reassumed the position.

"One more thing!"

Visibly frustrated, she peered over at him. "What?"

"If something happens when you're under and you get in trouble, remember to tug the rope twice."

"Yeah, I got it."

Before Huber could stop her again, Jessie clicked on her high-powered flashlight and dove off the ledge into the water. The surface rippled, seemingly surprised at being startled after so many years of peace. Huber could follow Jessie's beam of light as she made her way down the first few feet. The beam of light then disappeared out of sight as she moved deeper. Eagle Claw maintained a grip on the rope and fed her slack as she swam around. About ten feet away, her head popped out of the water.

"What do you see?" Hannah yelled.

"It's very dark. It's hard to see any—"

Before she could finish the sentence, she let out a small shriek and her torso was pulled beneath the surface by some kind of powerful force. Eagle Claw gripped the rope to keep it from slipping out of his grasp. Huber's heart hit the floor as he saw Eagle Claw struggling to reel in the rope as if he'd caught a giant shark.

"What's happening to her?" Alejandro shouted. "Someone help her!"

Whatever was pulling her in the water was strong enough that it was pulling the rope from Eagle Claw's powerful hands.

"Get the rope!" Scott yelled.

Collectively, everyone grabbed onto the rope before it ran out. Gritting their teeth, each person pulled with all their strength in a bout of tug of war with some kind of unnatural force. Despite their best efforts, the rope continued to slip through their fingers. Huber watched in horror as the end of the line escaped their grasp and fell into the water.

"*Hermana*!" Alejandro shouted.

Huber's instincts took over. Without thinking, he took a breath and dove off the ledge after the rope. As he plunged into the dark water, a frigid shock rattled his bones, but he forced his body to acclimate. The light on his helmet shined ahead as he kicked his legs and propelled himself forward. Darting his eyes in every direction, he couldn't see Jessie or the rope. Then, he saw it. The very end of the rope was being pulled through an underwater crevice along the cavern's wall. Huber swam toward it and grabbed on just before it escaped through the hole. As he gripped the rope, he was yanked forward at an alarming speed through the crevice. The friction caused him to shut his eyes, and he ducked his head to keep water from infiltrating his nostrils. He was a worm on a hook being dragged through the depths, perhaps bait for some kind of monster of the underworld.

Then, suddenly, the dragging stopped. He opened his eyes and realized his helmet had come free during the commotion. He was in pitch-black water. His chest pounded in panic as he swam upward but then realized that he wasn't sure if he was swimming upward or downward. He was going to drown! He scanned in all directions within the darkness. He noticed a small light somewhere ahead. He knew he had mere seconds before he gave into the temptation to breathe in the water. He kicked forward and the light enlarged. He was now confident he was swimming upward.

The light grew brighter and bigger like in his dream he'd had in the motel. Just as Huber opened his mouth to take a breath, he crested the surface and gulped in air. He grabbed onto a slick, rocky ledge and pulled himself upward, heaving and spitting out water. He was drenched and his body began to shake like a leaf. He knew he didn't have long before hypothermia set in. He looked around. The light he had seen coming through the water was Jessie's flashlight, which was resting on the ledge next to him, angled downward toward the water. He picked it up and swung it around the room. The ledge merged onto a small trail that led upward. Huber followed it and what he saw caused him to stop in his tracks. The rope was coiled into a perfect circle, like a snake ready to strike.

"Jessie!" Huber shouted. "Where are you?"

His voice echoed throughout the cavern. There was no response. He shouted over and over as he followed the trail, careful not to slip and fall back into the water below. Up ahead, Huber's light illuminated Jessie standing at a dead end. She was staring straight at him, but it was as if she didn't see him. She was looking vacantly beyond him.

"Jessie!" Huber shouted. He ran to her and grabbed her by the shoulders. They were stiff as rocks.

He waved his hands in front of her face, but she didn't blink.

"What happened? Can you hear me?"

She gave no response. Huber shook her, and her eyes met his. She whispered something and started repeating it louder and louder. They were words Huber couldn't understand. It was as if she were speaking another language.

"I can't understand what you're saying!"

She stopped abruptly, peered intently into Huber's eyes, and said, "All those who seek the Golden Staff, seek death." She smiled. "If you succeed, free us from its hold."

Jessie then collapsed into Huber's arms, unconscious. As she did, Huber saw a lever behind her. It was made from stone and carved into the wall. He pulled it downward, and a loud grinding noise shook the entire cavern. Huber looked behind him and over his shoulder. He shined his light upward and saw the other side of the golden door slowly opening fifteen feet above the path on which they stood. Moments later, Eagle Claw, Hannah, Scott, and Alejandro bolted through, shining their lights around the cavern.

"Help!" Huber croaked. "We're down here!"

● ● ●

After stripping down and wrapping himself in a

foil blanket, Huber had regained his body temperature and dressed in a set of dry clothes. Jessie was finally awakening.

Groaning and rubbing her forehead, she slowly came to her feet.

"What happened?"

"We were hoping you could tell us," Hannah said. "What do you remember?"

"I remember jumping in the water and looking around and then . . ."

"*¿Que? ¿Que pasó, hermana mía?*" Alejandro asked anxiously.

"Something grabbed me."

"What the heck was it?" Scott asked. "Thing was strong, that's for sure."

"I don't remember," she said groggily. "I'm not even sure I saw it. It's all a blank."

Huber approached her, still slightly recovering from the cold. "Do you remember what you said to me?"

Jessie looked up at him and shook her head. "No. What did I say?"

Everyone looked at Huber expectantly.

"Nothing. Just a bunch of weird stuff, like you were babbling in a different language." He chose to omit the other parts.

"Strange," Jessie remarked.

"What now?" Hannah asked.

"I say we go back," Alejandro said. "There is evil in this place."

Huber couldn't help but agree with him after what he'd witnessed, but he couldn't allow himself to give up the staff to the Brotherhood or Salazar.

"We've come too far, *hermano*," Jessie said. "We must continue our journey."

"What did Niza say we'd face next?" Hannah asked.

Alejandro retrieved the next entry from Niza's diary and read:

> *Sunday morning, April 16*
>
> *After overcoming the water obstacle, we camped overnight just beyond the golden door. We then pressed forward for maybe half a mile along the path until we came to a wide chasm, fifty feet in length. Its depth I could not rightly say because the bottom was not visible to our eyes. The Cíbolans must have constructed the way that led across. It was a flexible rope composed of animal hide of some kind, extremely durable and strong. Cupping our hands around the rope, we proceeded to swing our way across. When we had made half the distance, I felt a small tingle in my hair. Others felt it too. We were soon engulfed in a black wind. Three of my company, unable to withstand its strength, were peeled away from the rope and fell into depths unfathomable, their screams losing volume as they traveled downward. The black*

wind persisted the entire length of the rope. At last we reached the other side, grateful to have survived the darkness.

"Black wind?" Huber said, puzzled.

"That don't sound like a picnic," Scott foreboded and turned to Alejandro. "Your idea of trekking back ain't such a bad one, Rico."

"I hope the rope is still at the chasm," Eagle Claw said.

"Okay." Huber nodded to Eagle Claw. "Lead the way."

CHAPTER
· 8 ·

JUST AS NIZA'S ENTRY had described, they'd walked about half a mile before coming to the aforementioned chasm. Their hearts sank as they surveyed the distance across the gulf and realized the rope he had written about was long gone, probably having come loose hundreds of years ago.

"How are we going to get across?" Alejandro asked.

"Just get a real good runnin' start, Rico. I'll give ya a boost as ya jump."

"Funny, Cowboy."

"We still have the rope, don't we?" Hannah asked.

"Yeah," Huber responded. "But how are we going to anchor it to the other side?"

Eagle Claw stroked his chin. "I've got it covered."

From his pack, he retrieved some kind of pistol. In its tip was what looked like a harpoon.

"Is that a gun?" Hannah asked, a bit unnerved.

"No," Eagle Claw responded. "It's a harpoon pistol. Your grandfather packed it for just such an occasion. I'll attach the rope to the end of the hook, shoot it to the other side, and anchor it in the stone."

"Do you think it will hold?" Huber asked.

Eagle Claw sighed. "Let's hope so. I'll go first to ensure it's safe for the rest of you."

Eagle Claw attached the rope to the hook on the end of his pistol, used his light to aim carefully, and pulled the trigger. The pistol boomed, and the rope whizzed through the still air. A soft thud echoed through the chamber as the hook dug into the stone on the other side. Eagle Claw explained that as the hook entered the stone, its barbed claws would expand and lend support. Eagle Claw tugged the rope as hard as he could, and Huber heard the hook expand and clink into the rock. It seemed secure enough. Scott helped Eagle Claw tighten the rope and anchor it on their side.

"Okay," Eagle Claw said solemnly. "Wish me luck." He then gloved his hands, got down on his knees, and scooted out over the edge. The rope sagged beneath Eagle Claw's weight, but it held strong. Moving his way forward hand over hand, he had traversed about half the distance when he looked back and indicated it was safe for someone else to start the crossing.

"Any volunteers?" Hannah asked.

"I'll go," Alejandro said bravely, obviously trying to impress her.

"Hold up a sec, Rico. I'll go next," Scott countered.

While they were bickering, Huber observed Hannah put on a pair of work gloves from her pack. She was moving on the rope before the argument was finished.

"Hey!" Alejandro shouted and made his way to the rope. "Hold up!"

A few moments later, Eagle Claw had reached the other side and Hannah was nearly halfway across. Alejandro was a quarter of the way with Scott right on his tail.

Huber looked at Jessie, still a bit unnerved from their earlier encounter. "So, no sign of the black wind. Maybe it's out of order."

Jessie smiled. "Let's hope so. I'll go next."

"Are you sure?"

She nodded, gloved her hands, and made her way out onto the rope. Eagle Claw was helping Hannah up on the other side. Alejandro was three quarters of the way there and Scott was at the halfway point. Once Jessie reached the quarter mark, Huber ventured out onto the rope, forcing himself to not look down. It was like hanging on a telephone wire with no bottom beneath his feet. He had never felt more unsafe or less invulnerable. When he reached about a quarter of the way, he looked ahead to see Alejandro climbing his way up and Scott close behind him. Jessie was shimmying her way past the halfway point. Huber made the mistake of looking down at his feet dangling in the air and took a sharp intake of breath. The effect was dizzying. The sight of the depths brought upon him a sense of vertigo, but he mustered his strength and forced himself to move faster toward the other side. He was at the halfway point and Jessie at the three-quarters mark when he heard something, a high-pitched chirping ascending from below his feet.

"You hear that?" he shouted to Jessie and the others.

Everyone looked down into the darkness as the sound intensified. Huber had heard the sound before. He realized where just as a school of bats flew upward. They blanketed the air, slapping into his face and getting caught in his hair. There must have been thousands! It was the black wind! Huber even felt a few that had gone up his pant leg and were scratching around. He fought as hard as he could to not let go of the rope and swat them away.

It was too much. He freed one hand to shoo them away from his face.

When he did, he lost his balance and his other hand almost lost its grip. He swung his free hand upward and found the rope, wrapping his elbow around it. From below, the bats kept streaming upward, their nails digging into his neck. He shouted but was sure no one could hear him above the deafening sound. Not knowing how long it would take for the bats to move on, Huber forced his hands to keep moving. After what seemed like an eternity, a strong hand found him through the shower of bats and pulled him onto the ledge. Eagle Claw ushered him into a small cave to shelter him from the nocturnal nightmare. The others were cowering inside too. Huber caught his breath and could feel the many small scratches all over his body. He opened his pant leg and several bats flew out to join their company.

After a few more minutes, the last of the bats finally moved on. There must have been an opening to the outside world somewhere up above. Scott clicked on a flashlight and grimaced when he looked at Huber.

"How bad is it?" Huber moaned.

"Looks like you got in a fight with a herd of cats! Hope you got your rabies shot."

"Here." Eagle Claw handed Huber a bottle of distilled alcohol and some cotton swaps. "To make sure nothing gets infected."

Jessie and the others were cleaning their scratches too, though Huber seemed to have received the worst of it, having been in the thick of the storm.

Eagle Claw checked his watch and surveyed the small cave they were in.

"It's late. We should rest here for the night. We'll move on in the morning."

"How we supposed ta tell when it's morning in this place?" Scott asked.

"We'll take turns keeping watch two at a time to ensure no one is following. Scott and I will take the first shift, followed by Hannah and Alejandro, then Huber and Jessie. Two hours each."

"How come I get stuck with you and Rico gets paired up with Hannah?"

"Because I enjoy your company," he said, smirking, and then turned to the others. "Everyone get some rest."

Huber was so exhausted, he literally could sleep on a rock, and it seemed he would. From his pack he unrolled a thin sleeping bag and used some spare clothing as a pillow. It was uncomfortable, but he didn't care. He noticed Jessie lying across from him, her gaze far away. Ever since the incident in the water, she hadn't been quite herself.

"You okay?" Huber asked groggily.

She nodded absently. "Just tired."

"Well, see you in a few hours." He yawned and allowed his eyes to shut.

●　●　●

Walking along a sandy beach, Huber looked out over

the water and shielded his eyes against the blaring sun in a bright blue sky. Gulls were crying for food and circling in the air. The gentle lapping of the waves against the sand relaxed him. Off in the distance he could make out people waving to him. He squinted and realized it was Alejandro, Scott, and Hannah. He smiled and jogged his way to them. They were busy creating a sand sculpture of some kind.

Huber caught up to them.

"What are you guys up to?"

"Building a city out of sand," Hannah responded.

"Which city?"

"Which one do you think? Cíbola!"

Huber looked down at the sand sculpture they had created. It looked almost like a wheel. Along the wheel were six step pyramids equally spaced apart. On top of each were strange symbols: a feather, a sun, a crescent moon, a skull, a turtle, and a snake. In the center of the wheel was a step pyramid twice as big as those around the perimeter. Atop the pyramid in the center sat a man on a throne with an elaborate headdress and staff in his hand. It must have been El Dorado.

"Cool!" Huber said. "What are all those pyramids around the outside?"

"Temples of the sentinels," Alejandro answered. "Each one holds a key you'll need to get into El Dorado's Temple."

"This is a dream, isn't it?" Huber asked.

Scott grinned and answered. "You'd like to be on a beach right now, wouldn't ya? To go for a swim?"

The word *swim* brought the memories of Jessie and the water chamber flooding back into his mind.

"So, what's next?"

Everyone acted as if they didn't hear and kept sculpting their city of sand. As Huber peered closer at the figure representing El Dorado, he noticed the staff was now missing from his hands. From behind, he felt a dark presence. He did an about-face and saw Salazar, hair drenched and hanging in his face, clutching the Golden Staff. The villain flipped back his hair, and Huber looked into his eyes, absent of irises or pupils. The man grinned and tapped his shoulder with the staff.

Huber awoke with a start. Jessie was shaking him.

"Hey, it's our turn for watch. Are you okay?"

"Yeah," he said, rubbing his eyes. "Just a weird dream."

"You were snoring rather loudly. I didn't sleep much."

"Sorry."

Alejandro and Hannah were making their way back to the camp inside the cave, having spent the last two hours keeping watch. Scott and Eagle Claw were both asleep.

"See or hear anything?" Huber asked.

"Dead quiet," Hannah answered.

"Hopefully the Brotherhood and Salazar are still far from here."

At the moment, Huber didn't feel particularly concerned about either of their foes. His preoccupation was with Jessie. He couldn't quite put his finger on it, but something had changed about her. Huber stole a quick glance at her and couldn't help but wonder if they were dealing with terrors far beyond anything mortals could inflict.

● ● ●

The first hour had been uneventful. Huber had stood watch with Jessie in awkward silence, staring out over the chasm by the light of their lantern.

Finally, Huber decided to bring up the earlier events.

"So you really don't remember anything that happened back there?"

Jessie's voice was terse. "I told you. No!"

Huber sighed. "I think you do. Tell me what's going on with you."

A long moment passed, then she turned toward him, her tone more subdued.

"I honestly don't remember what happened, but since it did, every time I close my eyes, I see this image."

"What is it?"

"It's a face. A woman."

"Who?"

Jessie shook her head. "I don't know, but the deeper

we go, the stronger the image is, almost like getting closer to a radio signal. I fear we're all plunging headlong into some sort of trap we'll never be able to escape from. We were foolish to come down here. We should have stayed with *Abuelo* and let Salazar and the Brotherhood battle it out. I have a feeling they would never escape anyway."

"We can't take that chance. I'm sorry about what happened to your grandpa, by the way. I know that's probably weighing on you now more than ever."

Jessie slipped her hand into Huber's and said nothing. The moment was short-lived however, as a sound echoed across the chasm. Their fingers instantly separated, and Huber grabbed the lantern, holding it up high to lengthen his view.

"You heard that, right?"

"*Sí,*" Jessie replied. "It sounded like voices."

Huber strained his eyes in the darkness. A beam of light danced around the hole they'd come through on the other side.

"Someone is coming," Huber said.

"Turn off the lantern!"

Huber quickly switched off the lantern and absconded in the darkness. The light across the chasm grew brighter, and Huber could definitely hear people conversing.

"Go wake the others!" Huber whispered.

Jessie shuffled along to the small cave where everyone else was sleeping.

Suddenly, the light emerged from the hole on the other side. Huber's stomach dropped as he recognized the distinct voice of Juan Hernán Salazar.

● ● ●

"We have to move now!" Huber shouted as he entered the cave where everyone had been slumbering.

Jessie had already roused everyone, and they were busy packing things up.

"Salazar and Jack are coming!"

"Did you cut the rope?" Eagle Claw asked.

Huber's eyes widened. "No!"

Eagle Claw brandished a knife and retreated back to the chasm. Huber and the gang were on his heels. As they entered the chamber, Salazar and Jack were halfway across their makeshift bridge. The men looked up at Eagle Claw.

"*¡Hola, chicos. Hola, chicas!*" Salazar shouted across the way. "Very nice of you to leave us a crossing."

Eagle Claw brought the blade toward the rope.

"Please don't do that!" Salazar shouted. "Or my friend here will shoot you."

Huber held up the lantern to see Jack leveling a pistol toward Eagle Claw while holding onto the rope with his other hand.

"Leave the rope be!"

At that moment, Huber heard the sound he had heard earlier that night, but it was coming from above them instead of beneath. A trickle of bats were returning from their nocturnal meal.

Jack screeched as a bat grazed his head. "Ah, bats! I hate bats!"

"It's just a couple of flying mice! Stop whining!"

As Salazar finished his statement, the chasm instantly became a river of black. It must have been near dawn and the bat colony was returning to its nesting ground deep below. The torrent of bats continued for several moments. Huber and the others ducked behind their earlier-discovered crevasse and could faintly hear screams amid the flapping of wings. When the bats dissipated, Huber looked over the edge at the rope. Jack was gone. Salazar was hanging on and looked to be scratched up, just like Huber had been but maybe worse.

Bereft of firearms, Salazar looked at Eagle Claw pathetically and pleaded with him as he once again brought the knife toward the rope.

"Please, my friend, do not cut the rope. Allow me to cross and we will work together to find Cíbola. We'll share equally in its wealth. Just don't cut the rope, I beg you."

Eagle Claw kept the edge of the knife resting on the taut rope.

"What does everyone think?" he asked the group.

"Cut the thing!" Scott shouted. "It's no less than he'd do to you or me. Let him join his friend down below."

Salazar seethed at Scott's words but restrained himself.

"We've spared him before," Hannah said, "and lived to regret it."

Huber thought back to the cave at Dead Man's Treasure. He had shown mercy to Salazar, and in return, he'd almost lost his life. Salazar moved forward a few inches along the rope. "Do not forget, *jóvenes*, that it was I who helped you all escape the Brotherhood's castle in *España*."

"For your own purposes," Alejandro said. "You didn't care about us."

"Jessie? Huber?" Eagle Claw asked while keeping his eyes on Salazar. "What do you think?"

"I cannot murder a man," Jessie said. "Let him go back to the other side, then cut the rope."

"That'll just slow him down," Scott shot back. "Ain't gonna stop him."

"Yoo-ber." Salazar smiled at the boy and made his way a few inches closer. "We've been through so much together, you and I. Will you really let this man end my life?"

Huber looked upon his foe who had haunted his dreams for so long. "I won't let Eagle Claw cut the rope," Huber said and held out his hand to Eagle Claw.

The man reluctantly handed Huber the blade, giving him an unsure look.

Salazar was moving deliberately toward them now, albeit slowly, almost imperceptibly.

"But you told me that if you saw me or the others down here, it'd be the last time. Maybe you were right!"

Huber slashed the blade at the rope. The first hack set free the outer fibers but didn't sever the core of the line.

"No!" Salazar shouted and swung himself backward. "You will live to regret this Yoo-ber."

"You've got about ten seconds to get back to the other side before this thing snaps."

Salazar made a beeline back the way he had come, but he didn't make it back in time. The rope groaned and made a whooshing sound as it snapped. Salazar's eyes momentarily made contact with Huber's in one last fit of rage before the man fell, clinging to the middle of the rope. It swung toward the other end of the chasm with its passenger. Salazar's shoulder slammed into the stone wall, but he maintained his grip on the rope.

"Arrrgghhh," he yelped in pain and struggled to hang on.

Salazar dangled from the split end of the rope and planted his feet along the wall. He tried to climb his way up, but it seemed he couldn't do so with his shoulder injury.

The man panted in fatigue, and Huber knew it'd likely be mere minutes before the strain became too much and he let go of the rope.

"C'mon," Huber said to the others. "I don't want to watch."

Jessie glared at him as they made their way forward. Salazar's curses being spewed at them grew fainter.

"I cannot believe you did that! I never thought you capable of such a barbaric act! What kind of a person are you?"

"You know what he's done! What he would do to us if he had the chance!"

Scott came to Huber's defense. "Huber showed him mercy before and we all nearly got killed for it. Fool me once, shame on somebody. Fool me twice . . . I can't remember the rest, but ya know what I mean!"

"I hate to say it." Hannah shook her head. "But I think Huber did the right thing."

"I agree," Alejandro said.

"Then you are all guilty." Jessie stormed ahead of the rest of the group.

"Don't worry 'bout her, dude," Scott said. "She'll come around once she thinks it over."

Huber felt sick at what he had just done but felt he hadn't had a choice. He had to keep everyone safe, but maybe Jessie was right. Perhaps Salazar had turned him barbaric.

"Let's just keep moving. I don't want to think about it," he said.

They passed through the cave where they'd slept and

back onto a winding pathway of tunnels. In some places they were only able to walk single file, and then they came to a wide opening into another cavern.

Before they stepped inside the opening, Huber stopped them.

"Wait! Alejandro, what does the journal say to do next? I don't think we should walk in there blind. There could be some kind of trap waiting for us."

Alejandro nodded, then pulled out the diary and began to read.

Sunday afternoon, April 16

Pórtico de Oro

After passing through the black wind, we found ourselves staring into the dark void of a long chamber. One of the men related to me that in order to progress on our journey and enter the city, we would need to enter and pass by one more obstacle—the seven specters of death. I was not sure what he meant, and then he lifted his torch as we entered the chamber. The sight defied description and struck terror in my heart. Many of my men who had traversed to this point turned around when they laid their eyes on the scene. I was told it was a final warning to those who enter. I kept my eyes forward and walked through the valley of the shadow of death. I feared no evil and was delivered. The entrance to Cíbola was clearly marked and those brave men who dared follow entered the city with me. I was well rewarded as I stood before the gates to Cíbola—massive works of gold and iron—taller than twenty men. There was an inscription I could not read etched on the face of the gates along with a kind of a knocker, ancient in appearance. My guide told me that the inscription read that the key to opening the gates was a secret kind of knock. If done incorrectly it would result in our deaths. The inscription said to knock the number of days a man will live. My guide told me he knew the answer, but I wasn't so sure.

On another note, at this time, a strange sickness of the mind had begun to infect some of my men. They told me that they were seeing images of faces, hearing voices. Nonetheless, we pressed forward.

"He obviously made it through, so he must've figured out the riddle," Hannah said.

"Yeah, and didn't have the common courtesy of tellin' us the answer," Scott huffed.

"He wouldn't want to make it too easy for his readers, now would he?"

"Perhaps we should first worry about getting through that cavern up ahead and whatever is inside—the seven specters of death," Eagle Claw said solemnly.

Turning their lanterns as bright as they could, they prepared themselves to enter the darkness ahead. Eagle

Claw once again volunteered to go first. Huber stayed a few steps behind him. The darkness gradually gave way to the light of their lanterns.

Suddenly, Eagle Claw stopped in his tracks.

"What's wrong?" Huber whispered.

"Stay back. There are people up ahead of us. Several of them."

"What! Have they seen us?"

Huber watched Eagle Claw's frame as he continued to stare ahead.

"They're not moving. It's almost like . . . they're statues." Eagle Claw made his way forward.

As Huber followed, the vague outlines of people became visible. There were seven men standing in a perfect row, lined up like soldiers. As Eagle Claw and Huber neared the figures, he breathed a sigh of relief. They weren't moving. Apparently, they were statues of some kind.

Upon closer inspection, Huber realized they weren't just any kind of statues; they seemed to be sculpted of solid gold. Huber moved closer to the nearest statue to examine it up close, holding his lantern high. The statue he viewed appeared to be a man of average build, clothed in some kind of robe that came down to his ankles. His hair flowed past his shoulders and his palms were open and outstretched as if welcoming visitors. It was so life-like that Huber couldn't get past it. The light from his lantern danced off the sheen of the statue's face. It was then Huber noticed the expression the statue wore. It wasn't one of welcoming; it was panic, as if pleading for mercy. His mouth was open, trying to cry out words that would never come out. The statues to his side wore equal expressions of terror and fear.

Huber brought his free hand to the man's face and touched the cold, metal cheek. As he did, a jolt of electricity shot through him, and he saw the man's eyes move toward and lock onto his. He tried to cry out but couldn't. Images of people suffering and screaming flooded his thoughts, then silence reigned just as quickly. Huber pulled back his hand and stumbled backward. As he closed his eyes, he saw a faint impression, the same face he'd seen plastered over the earlier doorway—El Dorado. When he looked back upon the statue he'd just touched, the eyes were back in their normal position.

Huber watched as others approached the various statues. Jessie was hanging back, keeping her distance.

"Don't touch them!" Huber called out.

For Alejandro, Scott, Hannah, and Eagle Claw, it was too late. They seemed to be experiencing the same jolt as Huber and were reeling back.

"What the heck was that?" Scott rubbed his head. "It was like a bad dream, but it was real."

"It was like reliving someone else's memory," Hannah said.

It was then Huber realized that they weren't standing before statues.

"These were real people!" Huber shouted. "They must've been turned to this form by the Golden Staff."

Huber couldn't bear to look at their faces anymore and tried to force the images and sounds from his head.

"Did any of you hear voices?" Eagle Claw asked.

Huber knew what he was talking about but didn't want to say it out loud. It seemed Scott, Alejandro, and Hannah had heard too but weren't speaking up. Jessie then approached them.

"As we are, you shall be," Jessie uttered the words they were all thinking. "The words have been repeating over and over in my head since coming out of the water."

"I do not think we fully understand the forces we are dealing with in this place," Alejandro said. "Are we sure we want to go forward?"

"Did you forget?" Jessie said. "We can't go back. Huber cut our escape route."

"If Salazar had been allowed to cross, we wouldn't have made it this far, I promise you," Huber snapped defensively.

"We have no choice," Eagle Claw said somberly. "We must go on."

Passing the seven specters, they approached the massive iron and golden gates that supposedly led into the city. Built into the stone, they were arched and ornately carved.

In the center was the skull of El Dorado, the same image Huber now saw each time he closed his eyes. Attached to his face on the door was a nose ring that served as a knocker. Above the skull was the inscription Niza must have referenced.

"How many days does a man live?" Hannah pondered.

"That's an impossible question," Alejandro said. "The lifespan of every man and woman is different."

"If it were an average, it'd be in the tens of thousands," Huber said.

"That's a whole lot of knockin'." Scott whistled. "We'd be here for weeks. Not it!"

"We must think of the riddle as created by El Dorado," Jessie said. "From his culture and viewpoint."

"Does Niza's diary offer any other clues?" Eagle Claw asked Alejandro.

Alejandro shook his head. "No, the next entry appears to be from within the city itself."

For twenty minutes, everyone stood before the gates, no one daring to touch the knocker according to Niza's earlier warning.

"The longer we stay here, the more chance we give the Brotherhood to catch up," Hannah said. "We've got to try and get in."

"I've been thinking," Eagle Claw ventured. "Among many of the ancients in my tribe, there was a belief that a lifetime unto a man was merely seven days unto the gods."

"So you think we just need to knock seven times?" Huber asked.

Eagle Claw nodded. "Yes. Seven days, seven cities of Cíbola. The number seven seems to be a pattern, but I've been wrong before."

"We have to move," Hannah continued.

"Any volunteers? I have a feeling we won't be able to door ditch this one if we're wrong."

"I'll do it," Jessie said.

"No," Eagle Claw started. "I—"

Before anyone could protest further, Jessie strolled up to the menacing knocker upon the door, grabbed the nose ring, brought it backward, and swung it into the door seven times with surprising force. It was like a loud gong sounding throughout the entire cavern. Everyone braced themselves as they waited for the gates to open or a certain death from below or above. Huber darted his eyes around nervously. For a long moment, nothing happened. Then the floor of the cave began to vibrate.

Scott turned to Alejandro. "Hey, Rico, if we die in a few seconds, just remember what I told you."

"What's that, Cowboy?"

"UFOs are totally fake!"

Huber watched in relief as a crack of space materialized in the center of Dorado's face upon the gate.

"It's opening!" he yelled and turned to Eagle Claw. "You were right!"

Eagle Claw nodded in obvious relief.

The gate continued in a wide arc until both doors of the gate gave way enough for two or three people to enter at once. A musty, old odor whooshed through the opening.

"Well . . . ," Huber said. "We're here."

CHAPTER
· 9 ·

A SHAFT OF GOLDEN light reflecting somewhere from up above shone down upon the group as they entered the gate. Beyond the light, they couldn't see what lay ahead.

"Where's the light coming from?" Alejandro asked.

"Maybe it's a UFO about to beam us up," Scott responded.

"It has to be coming from the surface somehow," Eagle Claw said. "It's morning now."

Staring up into the light amid the swirling dust particles, Huber made out some kind of golden mirror reflecting the sunlight down on them.

"Look up there," he said, pointing it out to the others. "The light is being reflected down here through a mirror."

"The Cíbolans must've installed a series of mirrors

from the surface to have light down here. Ingenious," Jessie said.

As Huber stepped forward, he noticed the ground felt smooth where he stood. He tapped his foot and it made a hollow sound. Using his foot, he swished around the dirt.

"Hey, I think we're standing on something. Help me dust it off."

Everyone dropped to their hands and knees, dusting off the surface of the ground. As they did, it became clear they were standing on some kind of polished metal. Soon, Huber could see his reflection staring back up at him.

"It's a mirror, like the one above us."

"Some kinda lever over here!" Scott shouted. "Should I pull it?"

"No!" Eagle Claw shouted. "Don't pull any—"

It was too late. Scott had already pulled the stone lever upward out of the dirt. Something that sounded like gears rumbled beneath them.

"Off the mirror!" Huber shouted.

Everyone scattered off the surface. The mirror began to move upward and tilt at an angle. It was resting on a stone slab covered with etched symbols. As it tilted, it reflected the sunshine from above and shot it outward into the darkness. The slab slid to a stop, and as it did, a mirror somewhere far off in the distance caught the light and relayed it to a network of mirrors all around the vast cavern, illuminating the entire space in a dim, golden glow. A ticking sound echoed around them.

"It's a mechanized system," Jessie said. "The mirrors move with the sun."

"Whoever lived down here was very advanced," Eagle Claw marveled. "It's almost 9:00 a.m. We'll have about ten hours of light. After that, lights out."

"I seriously don't wanna wander through this place with just a lantern," Scott said.

"We had better get moving then. But, wow, just look at this place!" Alejandro responded.

Until this moment, no one had realized just how massive the room had been. They stood within a monumental arched dome. The space within was immense.

"This place must be over a hundred acres!" Hannah said.

As their eyes adjusted, the outlines of buildings became visible all around them. The faint sunlight reflected off water all around them. They were standing on one of many miniature islands within the cavern. In the center of each of the islands was a pyramid, glittering in gold.

"It's a lake!" Jessie said. "A huge underground lake."

In the center of the lake stood a large lonely island. Built upon it was a gigantic step pyramid, which almost reached the top of the dome. It glittered in gold like the others.

"I'm guessing that's where El Dorito lives," Scott said.

"How are we supposed to get there? Swim?" Alejandro asked.

Peering down into the water, Huber didn't want to guess what kinds of traps or surprises were just below the surface.

"No way," he said. "I'm guessing if any of us venture into that water, we won't come back out."

"I have a feeling you're right about that," Eagle Claw agreed.

"Amazing! Simply amazing!" Hannah said in awe. She observed the many golden adobe style houses and small buildings surrounding the pyramids on the islands. "What does Niza's journal say to do next?"

"He drew this place," Jessie said. "It makes more sense now. Niza labeled his drawing *Los Siete Templos de Cíbola*."

"Which means?" Scott shrugged.

"The Seven Temples of Cíbola," Huber answered. "All of the history books say that Coronado was searching for seven cities. Niza knew the truth! They weren't cities. They were temples! But you were right about one thing, Scott. Look here." He pointed at the center of the image they'd printed off earlier. "That huge one in the center is *El Templo del Dorado*."

"Look," Hannah pointed out. "Each of the temples has a name."

Huber observed the sketch. Surrounding the center

of *El Templo del Dorado* were the other islands with their smaller temples. Going clockwise at 1:00 was *El Templo del Sol*, 3:00 was *El Templo Lunar*, 5:00 was *El Templo de Quivira*, 7:00 was *El Templo de Vida*, 9:00 was *El Templo de Muerte*, and at 11:00 was *El Templo de Kachinas*.

"Jessie, can you translate the next part of the diary?"

Jessie retrieved the next image of Niza's journal and strained in the light to decipher the handwriting.

> *Monday afternoon, April 17*
>
> *We spent the afternoon surveying the golden city. There were a total of seven islands in the city of Cíbola, each with its own central pyramid. The islands were connected in a circle by a series of rock bridges. The one in the center was said to house El Dorado. However, to gain entrance, my guide told me we had to gain a key from each island guarded by Dorado's sentinels. At the time, we were unsure whether these sentinels were traps, puzzles, or men. However, we determined to go forward, obtain the keys, and gain access to the main temple of El Dorado. What exactly the keys were and how we would use them I was uncertain.*

Before Jessie could finish reading the entry, footfalls sounded from behind. Looking back, Huber saw a terrifying sight—a grimacing silver mask topped with a shiny steel conquistador-style helmet coming into full view. The man was dressed in finely etched armor and thick red robes. It was Matón and an army of his soldiers marching on the golden gate.

"Close the gate!" Huber shouted.

Collectively, everyone rushed to the gate. Huber, Hannah, and Scott shot to one side; Jessie, Alejandro, and Eagle Claw on the next. The gate must have weighed over a ton. Exerting all their strength, they pushed. The side with Eagle Claw moved faster and shut in place before Huber's side.

The Brotherhood was approaching quickly. They would reach the gate before it closed.

Eagle Claw locked eyes with Huber. "Get the staff! Do not fail!"

"What are you doing!"

Eagle Claw shot through the gate like a bullet, crashing into Matón. He was instantly swarmed with men. Alejandro and Jessie ran to Huber's side and helped close the other side of the gate. Huber could hear the struggle and tried not to imagine what was going to happen to Eagle Claw. The gate locked tight into place and the sounds faded. Everyone sat in stunned silence at what had just happened.

"How are we going to go on without him?" Hannah asked.

"We'll have to do our best," Alejandro said glumly.

"It's not going to take them long to figure out the riddle to open the gates."

"It might," Huber said. "The only reason we figured it out was because of Eagle Claw. He'll never give them the answer. He gave us a chance to find the staff. We need to use it."

Everyone nodded in somber agreement.

"We'll need to split up to save time," Jessie argued. "Huber and I will go clockwise. Hannah, Alejandro, and Scott will go counterclockwise. We'll meet in the middle and enter Dorado's pyramid together."

"I think that's a good plan," Scott agreed. "Who knows how much time we have before those rats find their way in."

Alejandro quickly divided up the images of Niza's journal. Huber and Jessie would take entries regarding *El Templo de Kachinas*, *El Templo de Muerte*, and *El Templo de Vida*. Hannah, Scott, and Alejandro would attempt to find the keys from *El Templo del Sol*, *El Templo Lunar*, and *El Templo de Quivira*.

Huber looked at his sister and got a sense of foreboding that it could be the last time he saw her. "Good luck, sis. Meet you in the middle."

She nodded, seeming to think the same thing.

CHAPTER
•10•

HUBER AND JESSIE TROTTED along the narrow bridge toward *El Templo de Kachinas*. The island was decorated with many tall, adobe-style buildings that seemed to be connected in one sweeping complex that nearly covered the whole island. As Huber touched the outside wall, he could tell they weren't made of mud; they were hard, thick, heavy, and clearly composed of gold. They stood before a wide, arcing entrance leading inside the complex. There was an inscription over the arch, covered with symbols and glyphs they couldn't decipher.

"Can you imagine how much wealth is inside this place?"

"I imagine more than both of our piggy banks combined," Jessie said.

"I guess it's best not to think about it. Quick, what does Niza say about this island?"

Jessie retrieved the image and used her headlamp to translate.

> *El Templo de Kachinas*
>
> *My guide tells me that this island contains many totems and figures representing the Kachinas or gods of the Cíbolans. This temple is the religious gathering place of the city. Upon the entrance was an inscription that my guide said roughly translated to: "Do not offend the other world." Two of the men in my company lost their minds obtaining the key that can be found on top of the temple within a kiva. Ahul has the key.*

"That's all it says?" Huber sighed. He was hoping to glean more details. "Do you have any clue what any of that means?"

Jessie shook her head. "I guess we'll find out."

They cautiously entered the complex. Once inside, Huber was taken aback by the extraordinary artwork and glyphs that decorated the inside walls. Clearly, this place was meant to inspire. Frescoes were everywhere he looked. He wished he could linger and try to understand the stories behind all of the drawings. They seemed to be in a commons area. It was eerie to be in such a large space with no people. There were several hallways leading off into different directions.

"I wonder how we get to the center of this place. Any ideas of which way to go?"

Jessie stroked her chin, then closed her eyes. As she did, she seemed to lose her balance and fall to her side. Huber was instantly there.

"Hey! Are you okay?"

Her body seemed to be trembling, then it suddenly stopped and her eyes opened wide. Huber recognized the trancelike stare from the earlier experience in the water-filled cavern.

She smiled, and when she spoke, her voice sounded lower and more guttural. "So, you seek the key of Ahul?" she asked.

"Jessie?"

"The one you call Jessie is temporarily away. I will be your guide to the temple."

"What are you talking about? Jessie, snap out of this!"

"Close your eyes," she said softly.

"Wait! Where is she?"

"Do it!" the voice snapped.

Huber briefly closed his eyes. As he did, the sharp image of a woman's face burned clearly in his mind.

"Who are you?" he asked in his mind.

"A guide from beyond," she said dreamily. "One of many who dwell here. If you do not seek Dorado's staff for gain or power, I will help you against those who do. I am called Tiwa."

"What will happen to Jessie?"

"She is safe and will return once my mission is complete."

"Mission? What is your mission?"

Jessie, or rather the one possessing Jessie's body, paused and brought her face closer to Huber. "To destroy the Golden Staff and be released from this tomb."

● ● ●

Huber had been following Jessie or rather Tiwa throughout the complex for around twenty minutes. They had navigated through corridors and ancient kitchens, and they were now coming upon the residential part of the complex.

"Prepare yourself," Tiwa said.

"For what?"

Huber didn't need a response as he walked through a doorway into a room filled with sleeping bodies. There was row upon row of inanimate people, frozen eternally in their peaceful state.

Tiwa pointed to one of the bodies. "That one there is me."

Huber looked upon the golden face of the woman sleeping peacefully. In her arms, she held a small child, also slumbering. Huber had seen a documentary once about the people of Pompeii, Italy. A volcano had erupted and covered everything, including the people in ash, forever freezing their frames in time. The sight of Tiwa and her daughter brought back those memories. Her features were pleasant and full as if she were having a good dream, but she would never awaken.

"Dorado or Lonan did this to you?" Huber said as a fact more than a question.

"Yes. He came in the night and touched us with his staff. We've all been here for so long. We've been watching you since you arrived in the cave."

"Are you able to see what's happening now? Do you know what happened to Eagle Claw?"

"There will be some who join our ranks into the netherworld this day. I am not at liberty to say who. To obtain the Golden Staff, sacrifice will be required."

"I've seen enough," Huber said. "Lead me to the temple."

Tiwa motioned. "This way."

Even Jessie's posture seemed to change as the one occupying her body led Huber onward through the residential center. He sighed heavily as he saw dozens of slumbering citizens lying upon their beds on the floor.

"Cíbola was a great city," she went on. "We were well hidden, secure, and had enough wealth so that we never wanted. At first, we reverenced Lonan as a benevolent leader, giving us our heart's desire. However, it didn't take long for everything to change. He became drunk with his power, and many others desired it for themselves. Everyone feared civil dissension and war. We became prisoners in our own city. My husband, daughter, and I planned to escape this place. But before we could, we were touched with the staff. We never awoke," she said somberly as they approached a doorway leading out of the residential portion of the complex. "Here we are—the Temple of Kachinas."

Huber brushed by Jessie and avoided making eye contact. He stepped out of the doorway into a plaza. In front lay the temple.

"Come with haste," Tiwa admonished and seemed to float up the temple steps.

Huber followed. A few short minutes later, they arrived to the top of the temple platform. In the center of the flat platform was a wide circle. Within the circle were a dozen or so totems or statues, ten feet in height of elaborate design. A tiny stream of water ran around the circle, but if the water moved, it was doing so at a pace that was imperceptible. The features on the Kachinas were symmetrical, were geometrical, and appeared to incorporate many elements of the earth and cosmos in their structure. Their colors were as vibrant as if they'd been freshly painted. Layers of orange, red, and gold were on some. Others were decorated with cool colors of blue, purple, and black. Huber had never seen anything like them. He wasn't sure whether they appeared intimidating or inviting, beautiful or terrifying. They were somewhere in between.

"Which one is Ahul?" Huber asked. "Niza said that's the one with the key."

Jessie or Tiwa pointed to the totem in the middle of the group and circle.

"So where is the key?"

"Why don't you ask him?"

"Ask who?"

Tiwa smiled. "Ahul."

"How am I supposed to talk to statues?"

"Go down to the stream, cup your hands, and drink the water."

"Drink the water? No way!"

"It is the only way you can communicate with Ahul."

"Are you sure that's safe? That water has been down here for how many years now?"

"It is the only way," she repeated.

Reluctantly, Huber stepped toward the circle of water. The Kachinas appeared even more massive up close. He cupped his hands in the water and brought them to his face. He turned to steal a glance at Tiwa, who nodded for him to proceed. Huber closed his eyes and gulped the water. Staring ahead at Ahul, he waited, but nothing seemed to happen.

"Speak to him," Tiwa called out.

"This feels so stupid talking to a totem pole," Huber

mumbled. "Though I guess I've been talking with a ghost, so what's the difference?"

He walked toward it. Its face was blue and divided into four quadrants. An upside-down triangle seemed to function as its mouth. A row of black-and-white feathers arced around its head, and the body was painted so that it appeared to have a long white robe. He touched the totem. As he did, the world around him swirled and everything fell away except him and the Kachina. It was as if they were suspended in outer space.

"Whoa," Huber said. "What was in that water? Where am I?"

The head of the Kachina rotated toward him, and the triangle moved as it spoke. "You have entered the realm of the Kachina," the low, wooden voice answered.

"Umm . . . I'm looking for Ahul. Are you him?"

"I am Ahul, the one you seek," the Kachina answered.

"I need your key to enter Dorado's Temple."

"For what purpose?" The voice became angry and shook Huber's bones.

"To destroy the Golden Staff of Cíbola."

"To destroy the staff!" Ahul laughed and shook the air. He then whispered, "The staff will destroy you."

The totem grew in size and towered over Huber. The Kachina lifted its hand and plucked a feather from its head, then handed it to Huber.

"Look up! Remember my words and avoid the staff's allure."

Huber looked upward. Above the Kachina, six white squares appeared in the blackness. The symbol of a feather appeared in the fourth square. The other squares remained blank. Huber let go of the statue and instantly he was back inside the circle on top of the temple platform.

"Whoa!" he said and stared up at Jessie, or Tiwa, who was watching him. "That was one of the strangest things to ever happen to me."

"Did he give you the key?"

"I guess so. I'm not sure exactly what it all meant. There were six squares in a row and the symbol of a feather was in the fourth one."

"Yes." Tiwa smiled. "You have obtained one of the keys. Let us move on to the Temple of Death." She pointed to the adjacent island and the stone bridge that connected it to the island on which they stood. Then Jessie suddenly collapsed.

Huber ran to her and shook her by the shoulders. It took a few moments, but finally, she stirred.

"Huber?" she said. "Where are we? What just happened?"

"I'll explain on the way. I have the first key. We need to keep moving."

CHAPTER
•11•

HANNAH, SCOTT, AND ALEJANDRO stood before *El Templo del Sol*—the Temple of the Sun. They had passed through a series of residential areas whereupon they viewed the sleeping golden forms of Cíbola's former inhabitants. It felt surreal to walk by their cooking and living areas. Many toys were still strewn about for children that would never play with them again. They'd even passed through a kind of unfinished construction site meant to expand the living areas. Until then, Hannah had been convinced that all the tales she'd heard about Lonan and Uhepono were just myths. Now, she knew they were true. After winding their way through the various small streets and residences, they had found themselves at the bottom of a step pyramid. A small pool of black liquid bubbled a few feet from the base of the pyramid.

"What is that?" Alejandro asked.

Hannah walked to the pool and inspected it more closely. "It's a tar pit," she said. "It was probably here for thousands of years, before the city was even built."

"We don't have time for a science lesson. What do we do now?"

Hannah directed her attention away from the tar pit and toward the pyramid. From her viewpoint, Hannah could see that resting on top of the pyramid was one of the relays that was reflecting the outside light around the cavern. The steps were narrow and steep, but seemed to be solid.

"Well, shall we head up?" Alejandro asked.

"Let's do it," Scott said. "Race ya to the top!"

"Hold on," Hannah cautioned. "Alejandro, read Niza's entry before we go up, just to be safe."

Scott moaned. "We ain't got time to be safe. In case you didn't notice, the Brotherhood is right on our tails."

"Yeah, and if we fall into some kind of trap, we'll be dead, won't we? The Brotherhood won't really matter then."

"Fine! Rico, read the thing!"

Alejandro pulled out the image of Niza's journal regarding *El Templo del Sol* and began to translate:

> *El Templo del Sol*
> *We climbed the steps leading to the top of the Sun Temple. We obtained the key from this sentinel, but had to withstand some physical strain and one casualty.*

"You better stay down here then, Rico."

"Be quiet, Scott! Keep reading, Alejandro!"

> *Once we reached the top of the temple, we found
> an inscription that advised a seeker to obtain the key
> by staring into the sun for ten breaths, or ten seconds
> I guessed. My guide stared longer and lost his vision.*

"Awesome," Scott breathed. "Too bad we didn't bring our sunglasses."

"Let's head up," Hannah said and stepped onto the first step.

As she put her weight on the step, a rumbling sound echoed around them.

"What'd you do?"

"I didn't do anything. I just stepped on the pyramid."

Slowly, the narrow steps of the golden pyramid turned inward until the steps disappeared and the surface became a slick, flat slope at nearly a forty-five-degree angle.

"*¿Que pasó?* How are we supposed to get up there now?" Alejandro wondered aloud.

Hannah believed she now knew why the entry said a person would need physical stamina.

"We're going to have to run up the slope. Just don't stop or you'll slide back down to the bottom."

"Ready for that race, Rico?" Scott shouted and bolted up the side of the pyramid

Alejandro was right behind him. Hannah watched

in amusement as Alejandro evened up the race and they neared the halfway point. She could tell they were struggling. Soon they both slowed to a walk and then their momentum stopped altogether. They came sliding backward on their bellies toward the foot of the pyramid. Scott landed in front of Hannah's feet, and seconds later, Alejandro toppled over him.

"Get off 'a me." Scott shoved him, straining to catch his breath.

Alejandro was also winded. "Just give me a minute. Let me breathe."

"Little harder than you thought, I see?" Hannah said, trying not to laugh.

"Why don't you give it a try?" Scott said between breaths. "Think ya could do better?"

"None of us are going to get more than halfway up running. It's impossible. We'll just tire ourselves out more each time."

"What do you think we should do, Hannah?" Alejandro asked.

Hannah rubbed her temples, scrambling her brain for a strategy to reach the top of the pyramid. A thought popped into her head, and she sprinted toward the temple's adjoining tar pit. She knew how she would reach the top. She stooped and came face to face with the black, bubbling liquid. Taking a breath, she plunged her hands into goo. The tar was warm, just above room temperature.

"Hannah! What are you doing?" Alejandro ran to her side. "Does it not burn? It's boiling!"

Hannah pulled her hands out and smiled. "It's not boiling at all. The bubbles are caused by bacteria eating the petroleum and gassing off methane as by-product."

Scott joined the two of them. "So you're saying there are little orgamisms that live in there and they're burping up those bubbles after they've stuffed themselves?"

"In a manner of speaking, yes. And they're organisms with an 'n' not *orgamisms*."

"That's what I said!"

Hannah shook her head and approached the temple steps, her arms dripping in tar.

"We'll run up as far as we can, then try to crawl the rest of the way. The tar will help us gain some traction and keep us from slipping."

The boys reluctantly dipped their hands in the thick substance and joined Hannah at the temple's base.

"Ready? Go!" Hannah shouted and was off like a bullet.

She knew she got a jump on the boys and didn't even bother to look over her shoulder. She reached the halfway point when her knees began to wobble. Hannah pushed herself as hard as she could and gained a few feet on the boys, then dropped to her hands. The tar did the trick and gave her just enough grip to keep herself from backsliding as long as she kept her feet kicking. She moved hand in front of hand and began to make slow progress toward the shining beacon at the top.

With each move forward, the gravitational pull became stronger, and she found herself gritting her teeth. She couldn't allow herself to stop kicking her feet, or there was no doubt she'd slide back toward the ground. From this height, she feared her speed would be so great she'd be injured when she finally hit the bottom. She couldn't afford to look back and see where Scott and Alejandro were. She had to keep moving forward.

As she neared the lip of the platform, her arms and legs finally gave out, and she collapsed, pressing her body as hard as she could against the cold, hard surface and hoping she didn't fall backward. She was within a few inches of the platform, but most of the stickiness of the tar had worn off of her hands. With one final effort, she pushed herself forward and her fingers caught the lip of the platform. She was then easily able to pull herself the rest of the way up to the roof of the pyramid. She lay there for a few minutes catching her breath, then stood to check on Scott and Alejandro's progress. They were still standing toward the bottom.

"Nice work, Hannah!" Scott shouted. "You made it!"

"You didn't even try!"

"We decided to stay here in case you fell so we could catch you."

"Yeah, right! You were just being lazy!"

"Well, you made it, didn't ya? Now get the key!"

Hannah shook her head at them in disgust. However, she did feel a sense of pride that she was the only one who made it up. She stood up and had to shield her eyes from the mirror reflecting sunlight to the next relay. It was ticking and slowly turning to the right, moving with the sun. Below the mirror, in front of her feet, was an inscription in Cíbolan. Recalling the advice from Niza's diary, she repeated the words to herself. "Stare into the sun for ten breaths."

Hannah peered up at the mirror and stared. She struggled to maintain her gaze at the bright object. She stared ahead, not blinking, and took even breaths. Three times, four, then five. Her eyes were watering like sprinklers. Six, then seven. Finally, she reached ten, closed her eyes and turned away from the mirror. As her eyes were closed, an impression seemed to burn onto the back of her eyelids. There were six squares in a row. All were empty except the second one, which contained a symbol. She had seen it many times before on the highway. The same symbol was plastered on all of the New Mexican license plates. It was a sacred symbol for Native Americans—the Zia Sun. She had read about the symbol in one of the books at the hotel. It had been around for thousands of years and represented life. The sun gave life to the people and the four lines signified birth, childhood, middle age, and elderly years just as the seasons changed from spring to summer, to fall, and to winter before repeating the cycle.

As her eyes slowly adjusted to the dimness of the cavern again, Hannah wondered how she would get down from the pyramid.

From below, Scott yelled toward her. "Did you find the key or what?"

"Yes! I have it. At least I think I do!"

"Hannah, how will you get down?" Alejandro called out.

Hannah slid her legs over the edge of the pyramid.

"Just be ready to catch me!"

MORGANTOWN PUBLIC LIBRARY
373 SPRUCE STREET
MORGANTOWN, WV 26505

CHAPTER
•12•

HUBER AND JESSIE HAD made their way across the next section of the bridge and reached *El Templo de Muerte,* or the Temple of Death. As they entered the area, it became obvious that this place wasn't used as a residence. It was a graveyard.

The area was adorned in memorials that were unlike anything Huber had seen. Intricate symbols and patterns of stone surrounded them. In the middle of the island stood this island's pyramid. Resting on top, Huber could make out a box of some kind.

They passed by a massive mound of stones on their way to the pyramid. Perhaps an old ruler or king of Cíbola had been buried there. The place was deathly still, but Huber sensed eyes watching him and ears listening.

Jessie, still recovering from her lapse in memory and struggling a bit physically, came to Huber's side.

"This place feels sacred. Like we don't belong."

"I know," Huber admitted. "I get the feeling we're not welcome. Let's read what Niza had to say and then get out of here."

Jessie removed the next image of the diary.

El Templo de Muerte

Only one of my guides would venture onto this island with me. The others dared not, stating if they accompanied me, a curse would follow them and their family. My guide and I made our way through the burial mounds and to the pyramid in the center. After reaching the top of the temple, we found a golden sarcophagus with an inscription upon it. My guide told me the translation roughly says, "I fall from above or climb from below; I creep in with time or surprise in the night; I cause mothers to weep and elderly to rejoice; I come to all and all come to me. To find the key to immortality, you must face me."

"Interesting," Jessie said. "Let's climb to the top and see if we can figure out what it all means."

The two of them ascended the pyramid. The climb was steep, but soon they had reached the platform at the top. Sure enough, there was a golden sarcophagus waiting for them. The golden box was covered in Cíbolan glyphs and symbols. The inscription Jessie had read about was on the side of the coffin.

"You must face me," Huber repeated to himself.

"It's obvious who the riddle is referring to, isn't it?" Jessie asked.

Huber nodded. "Yeah. Death. I think we have to open this thing and face what's inside."

"I get the feeling we're not going to like what we find."

Huber and Jessie stooped below the edge of the sarcophagus.

"Ready? One, two, three, push!" They pushed with their shoulders

The vein on Huber's head throbbed as he and Jessie pushed for all they were worth. The lid didn't budge.

Out of breath, they both collapsed and rested their backs against the box.

"It's too heavy," Jessie sighed.

Just then Huber noticed a lever sticking out of the floor near the foot of the sarcophagus. "Look at that," he said.

They approached the lever to inspect it more closely.

"What do you think it does?"

"One way to find out," Jessie said and pulled the lever toward her.

The sarcophagus rumbled as the middle of the lid popped up like a tent. The left and right pieces separated and slowly slid away, tucking themselves against the length of the box like a bird expanding its wings, then hemming them to its side.

Huber steeled himself and peered down into the coffin,

not sure of what to expect. To his amazement, there were no remains inside. It was just an empty sarcophagus.

"What do you make of this?" Huber asked.

"I do not know. Is there anything written on the inside?"

They surveyed the inside of the box but found nothing but smooth, polished edges.

Huber sighed and rubbed his temples. "You must face me . . ."

Jessie appeared equally perplexed.

Huber suddenly perked up. "I think I may have an idea," he said. He hopped up and squeezed himself inside the sarcophagus.

"Huber, what are you doing? Are you crazy?"

Huber lay flat inside the box, half of his face visible to Jessie.

"Okay, when I give the word, slide the lid back until it's closed."

"You are crazy!"

"*You must face me!*"

"What?"

"The riddle. It said the seeker would have to face death. I think that's what it means."

"Are you sure?"

"No . . . ," Huber hesitated. "But it's worth a shot. Just be ready to open it back up."

Jessie nodded. "Okay."

Huber took a deep breath. "Okay, close the lid."

Jessie made her way to the other side and slid the lid of the sarcophagus until it blocked out all of the light.

Inside the box, there was nothing but darkness and a silence so deep Huber had never experienced. He tried to fight the temptation to panic. His heart beat wildly. He wondered if he had made a mistake.

"Okay, Jessie." He knocked on the lid. "Open it back up. I must've been wrong."

There was no sound or movement from outside.

"Jessie?"

The air was getting hard to breathe now. "C'mon, Jessie! Open up!" He pounded.

The full effect of panic racked his body now. Huber pushed and kicked the lid for all he was worth, but it wouldn't budge. He started hyperventilating and couldn't figure out why Jessie wasn't opening the sarcophagus. Huber took one last breath as sweat poured down his face, then felt himself losing consciousness. He was going to suffocate and die in this box.

● ● ●

Up ahead in the darkness, Huber noticed a pinprick of light. Slowly, it grew bigger to the size of a baseball, then a beach ball. He was moving toward it fast. Before he knew it, he was enveloped in white. It was so bright, he had to shield his eyes. When he brought his hands down and his eyes adjusted, Huber surveyed his surroundings. He was standing at a riverbank running through a mountain valley. The sky was crystal blue, hills were lush and beautiful, and the gentle lullaby of the river and chirping of crickets put him at ease.

He inhaled the fresh mountain air and relaxed. Downstream, he noticed someone fly-fishing. Even before he saw the man's face, he knew it was his Grandpa Nick. Lying on the bank next to him was a fishing pole, all baited and ready to go.

Huber ran and picked up the pole.

"Hey, Grandpa!"

"Hey, *muchacho*." The man turned to his grandson and smiled. "How have you been?" Grandpa Nick clapped him on the shoulder.

"Better than I was a few minutes ago. I'm dead, aren't I? I suffocated back in that box back there."

Grandpa Nick floated his fly over the water. "I'm not exactly sure, but it's sure good to see you again."

"You too."

"So tell me about your quest."

Huber related his experience of trying to find the Golden Staff of Cíbola and his progress to the point before he had died.

"Pity you came so close." Grandpa Nick shook his head. "I can only imagine what will happen when that staff falls into the hands of those wicked men."

"Maybe Hannah and the others can stop them." Huber shrugged and floated his fly over the river.

"I'm afraid not, my boy. This task was meant for you."

"Well, there's nothing I can do about it now."

Grandpa Nick smiled at Huber and winked. "Well, you have a choice to make, see? You can choose to stay here or go back. It's up to you."

Huber had never wanted to stay anywhere more than the place he stood now.

"What will happen to the others if I stay here?"

Grandpa Nick pointed to the water. "See for yourself."

Huber peered down into the water. It was like watching a movie in reflection. He watched in horror as Fausto, wielding the Golden Staff, touched Alejandro, Jessie, Scott, Hannah, and then his parents, turning each of them to gold inside the city.

Huber dropped his pole. "I have to go back," he said without hesitation.

"I was hoping you'd say that."

"But I don't have the key!"

"Throw your line out over the water."

"But I've got to get back. I don't have time to fish."

"Just trust me."

Huber picked up his pole and threw his fly over the water. As it grazed the water, a huge trout gulped it up. Huber set the hook and began to reel.

"Nice work, my boy. Reel him in!"

The fish was strong and pulled hard. Huber was afraid the line would break any second. After battling for a few moments, he pulled the fish out of the water, but it was no longer a fish; it was a golden skull. Huber unhooked it and held it skyward. As he did, a series of six boxes appeared in the clouds. Huber held up the skull and instinctively knew it belonged in the third box.

"Looks like you caught your key!"

Huber smiled at his grandpa, dropped the skull, and gave him a hug. As he did, the world spun and he plunged back into darkness, coughing wildly. A sliver of light appeared and the sound of grinding metal filled his ears. Jessie's face appeared over him.

"Hey, are you okay?"

Huber gasped, inhaled air, and then crawled out of the box.

"What took you so long?" he hacked. "Why didn't you open the box when I asked you?"

Jessie looked at him confused. "You never said anything."

"I was kicking and screaming!"

Jessie shook her head. "No. You were quiet as a mouse. I finally got worried and just decided to open it up. What happened?"

Huber rubbed his head. "I faced death. And chose to come back. I have the key!"

CHAPTER
•13•

HANNAH, SCOTT, AND ALEJANDRO had made their way to the next island in search of *El Templo Lunar* or the Lunar Temple. Just like the island before, this too had a step pyramid centered in the middle. And just like the others, residences full of golden slumberers surrounded the perimeter.

"Hey, Rico, what does the next entry tell us to do?"

Alejandro retrieved the corresponding image and translated:

> *El Templo Lunar*
> *The temple loomed in the center of the island. Reaching the top was easy and solving the puzzle was moderately difficult. However, getting down from the pyramid was by far the most difficult part. One of my men lost his life on the way down.*

On top of the pyramid, we came upon a celestial puzzle. The Cíbolan inscription gave the following clue: "There are stars in the heavens, but there is no heaven here."

"And that is all it states," Alejandro said dejectedly. "Any ideas?"

Hannah repeated the phrase to herself and then asked the question, "Where is there no heaven?"

"I do not know," Alejandro said.

"Scott?"

"Ain't no heaven where we are, that's for sure."

Hannah thought for a moment, then exclaimed, "That's it, Scotty! Nice work!"

"Thanks, I s'pose. But for what?"

"There are stars in the heavens or in the sky, but no heaven or sky beneath the ground. The underground or underworld!"

"You might be right, Hannah," Alejandro said. "But how does the answer help us?"

"I don't know. Let's get to the top and find out."

The trek to the top of the pyramid was easy enough. Upon reaching the platform at the top, Hannah noticed a golden table with a dozen or so squares sticking up out of it. Each was about two inches by two inches and contained a symbol—Cíbolan glyphs. It appeared that the objective was to push in whichever square corresponded with the riddle.

"Anyone know what any of these symbols mean?" Alejandro asked.

Hannah scanned the symbols of reptiles, animals, stick-figure men, and others that were unlike anything she'd ever seen. "They all appear so foreign. I have no clue."

"Why don't we just push them all in? We're bound to find the right one," Scott suggested.

"Do you really think that some horrible thing isn't going to happen to us if we choose the wrong one?"

Scott shrugged. "So whatta we gonna do then, guess?"

Hannah analyzed each stone square carefully.

"There are no heavens here . . . which one looks like it most represents the underworld?"

"I dunno. They all look pretty weird to me."

Hannah had to agree. Each square had a figure upon it, and without being knowledgeable in this Zuni-Cíbolan language, she had no way to guess accurately. She wished Malia was with them. Perhaps she could shed some light on the subject.

"Look there," Alejandro said, pointing to a square. "That one looks like a devil. Perhaps it represents the underworld."

"I don't know if this culture associated horned devils with the underworld. That's more of a European way of thinking."

"Heck, it's worth a shot," Scott said and came forward.

"Scott, don't!" Hannah leaped to stop him, but it was too late.

Scott pressed the square containing the man with the horned figure. It slid down until it was flat with the table. A rumble sounded beneath their feet.

"Scott! What have you done?"

"I dunno! Why didn't ya stop me?"

The ground beneath their feet shook, and for a moment, Hannah was sure the pyramid would crumble and they'd be buried in rubble, suffering a horrible death through suffocation. She peered over the edge of the platform and watched in horror as each step of the pyramid flipped around row by row, revealing thousands of nasty golden spikes on the other side. Each spike was the same height and equidistant from the other. There would be no escape from the top of the pyramid. As the step closest to the platform flipped around, the rumbling stopped.

"Great job, Scott!" she shouted and threw her arms in the air. "Any idea how we're going to get down now?"

"I'll think of somethin'. Just give me a minute."

"Just don't press anything else!"

Alejandro tried to ease the tension. "Perhaps if we select the correct square, the steps will flip back around to their normal position."

"He better hope so!" she smoldered.

Hannah returned to the table and strained her mind

as she kept staring at the strange symbols. Her eye was attracted to a figure that in her mind appeared a bit like Bigfoot. The figure was woolly and had huge eyes. Hannah then remembered something she'd read in one of the books regarding the Zuni culture. Uhepono, the demon of the underworld who gave Lonan the Golden Staff, was rumored to wear a thick skin of wool and had huge eyes to watch those around him.

"I think I found the right one," she said to the others. "I can't be sure . . ."

"Do it," Alejandro said confidently.

"Don't care," Scott said, shrugging. "We're stuck up here anyway."

Hannah laid her finger over the figure and closed her eyes. She applied pressure and exhaled as the square went down. She cringed, waiting for something terrible to happen. There was no rumbling or any sound at all.

"Maybe the thing is broken," Scott said. "It is pretty old."

Suddenly, all of the squares of the table dropped simultaneously. Beneath the surface of the table, there was noise as if the squares were being shuffled around. In the middle row, six squares popped up at the same time. All were blank except the first one that contained a crescent moon.

"That's it! The moon is the key and it belongs in the first box. I'm starting to think each of these symbols we're finding are keys that belong in some sort of combination. That must be what opens the doors to Dorado's Temple."

Hannah pushed the crescent moon back in. As she did, the blank squares also dropped down, and within a few seconds all of the original squares popped back up into their original positions. Hannah smiled. "We did it!"

"Hate to be the bearer of bad news," Scott said. "We may have the key, but those spiky things are still there." He pointed over the edge.

Hannah's heart sank. They'd found the key from the Lunar Temple, but would be stuck on top of the pyramid forever.

"Wait! I have an idea!" Alejandro said and began digging in his pack.

He retrieved a long sleeve shirt and put it on along with his gloves.

"Cold or somethin'?" Scott asked.

"Just wait and see, Cowboy." He smiled.

To Hannah's utter disbelief, Alejandro flung his pack over the edge of the platform. Because of the angle of the pyramid, his pack cleared the spikes and thumped on the ground far below. Alejandro then placed his legs over the edge and laid flat on his back over the spikes.

Hannah squealed and brought her hands to her mouth. "Alejandro! What are you doing? Are you okay?"

She peered over the edge to see Alejandro smiling up at her.

"I'm fine. It's just like the bed of nails trick."

"The what?"

"I remember seeing a magic show in Salamanca. A magician lay flat on a bed of nails without harming himself. Because all of the nails were so close together and the same height and weight, the man's weight was distributed evenly. So it is here. Plus the texture of the spikes will keep you from sliding down."

Carefully, Alejandro rolled onto his belly, keeping his face up, then onto his back again, making his way down a few feet ever so slowly.

"It's quite nice actually, a bit like a massage. Just cover up your skin."

"Well, looky there. The Spaniard actually did somethin' useful on this trip. Guess I'm glad we kept him around."

Scott and Hannah followed Alejandro's instructions and made their way onto the spikes. It took some time, but eventually they reached the bottom of the pyramid unharmed. Each retrieved their pack and looked forward toward the next pyramid. It would be the last one before they met up with Huber and Jessie.

"*El Templo de Quivira*," Alejandro said.

Hannah smiled. "Let's find that last key!"

CHAPTER •14•

"ONE LAST KEY BEFORE we meet up with the others," Huber said hopefully as they stood before the entrance to the next island, which contained *El Templo de Vida,* or the Temple of Life.

"Let's hope this key is a little easier to get than the last one."

They entered the island and observed that this section of the city must have been the commercial center. Huber wondered what the marketplace would have looked like in the days when people lined the streets, trading and buying. While all of the perishables had long since vanished, many of the outposts still had jewelry and weapons, and even some remnants of animal hides were still displayed, waiting to be sold.

The main road led through the marketplace and ended at the pyramid temple in the middle of the island, just like the others.

As they approached the temple, Jessie retrieved Niza's next entry.

> *El Templo de Vida*
>
> *After working our way through the marketplace, we hiked our way up to the top of the temple. At the summit of the temple rested an alter containing an inscription. My guide translated the message from Dorado as follows:*
>
> *"I sustain and destroy. I give life and take away."*
>
> *After some time, we were able to decipher the inscription's meaning and obtain the key.*

Huber sighed. "Well, that's helpful."

"We'll figure it out," Jessie said confidently.

Huber and Jessie traversed their way up the golden pyramid, and just as Niza had indicated, there was a golden, ornately decorated altar at the top with an inscription over its face.

"Now we get to try and figure out what that inscription means," Huber said, staring at the flat stone altar.

Jessie repeated the phrase, then asked the question. "What sustains life and takes it away?"

"Time?"

Jessie nodded. "Yes, maybe. That could be it."

Huber shook his head. "I don't know. Even if I'm right, I'm not sure how that helps us here."

Stumped, the two of them took a seat at the top of the pyramid and looked over the city for several minutes. Off in the distance, the golden gate stood in stark contrast to the dark walls of the cavern.

Huber momentarily changed the subject. "How long do you think we have until the Brotherhood finds their way in?"

"It won't be long before they find their way in," Jessie said. "I'm surprised they haven't yet."

"What if we don't get to the staff in time?"

"We will."

"What happens if we can't destroy it? I mean, how would you even go about destroying some kind of mystical object like that? I'm guessing it won't be as easy as smashing it with a hammer."

"No, I imagine you are right. If we can't destroy it, we should hide it somewhere no one will ever find it."

"People like the Brotherhood are resourceful. I'm guessing even if we threw it in the middle of the ocean, they'd find it somehow. There's no limit to the pains they'd go through or blood they'd spill."

Jessie snapped her fingers. "That's it!"

"What's it?"

"I think you just solved the riddle!"

"I did?"

Huber looked at her, puzzled.

"When you talked about the ocean! Water! It sustains life and takes it away!"

Huber nodded but then asked, "How does water take away life?"

"Floods, hurricanes, drowning. There's many ways."

"So maybe the key is only revealed with water!"

Jessie yanked out her canteen and poured some water over the altar.

They waited for something to happen. After several moments, both sighed.

"It was worth a try," Huber said.

"Wait!" Jessie said.

As the water sunk into the altar's porous surface, it began to reveal a picture of some kind.

He took out his own canteen and drizzled more water over the altar. The picture became clearer. There were six boxes. The first five were empty, but the last one contained what looked like a turtle.

"It makes sense," Jessie said. "I remember reading about Zuni and Hopi beliefs. They believed the turtle had the power to bring rain."

"*El Templo de Vida.* Water brings life! We found the key!"

"Let's head to the rendezvous point and meet up with the others. I hope they've found their three keys too."

As Jessie finished her sentence, Huber heard the

sound he had been dreading. From their vantage point, they both looked back toward the entrance to the city and saw the gate swinging open.

Huber turned to face Jessie. Neither could hide the worry etched in their faces. "We better hurry. The Brotherhood is here."

•15•

HANNAH, SCOTT, AND ALEJANDRO were just entering the island containing *El Templo de Quivira* when they heard the golden gate opening.

"What do we do?" Alejandro began to panic.

"We stay calm," Hannah advised. "It will take them a little while to find their way to where we are. We need to find the last key quickly and get to Huber and Jessie. Maybe we can beat them to Dorado's Temple."

"Well, we best quit yappin' about it and get to it then," Scott said, and he began to jog toward the center pyramid.

Quivira seemed to be a training island for combat. Everywhere Hannah looked, she observed what appeared to be arenas and corrals. Scattered throughout were ancient weapons like spears and knives fashioned from bone. Others were either made of gold or must have been converted to the element by the staff. Hannah could almost see and hear the men in their dances of war and training.

"Quick, Rico!" Scott called out while they were on the run. "What does that priest dude say to do next?"

Alejandro pulled out the next entry and called for them to stop for a moment while he translated.

"Here is what Niza says:"

> *El Templo de Quivira*
>
> *We found Esteban at the top of the pyramid. My friend had perished in the process of trying to obtain the key from Quivira. My guide tells me we will suffer the same fate should we proceed incorrectly. Beneath Esteban's body was an inscription upon the floor. It reads that "he who seeks the Golden Staff must choose the deadliest of all weapons."*
>
> *I would have shared in Esteban's fate had my guide not been there to advise me of the correct answer.*

Galloping past the ruins and relics of a bygone era, the trio bounded up the steps of the pyramid. From the height of the steps, they could see a large mass of Brotherhood goons approaching, their lights and lanterns seemingly infinite. Half were on the bridge going toward the first island containing the Sun Temple. The other half were headed in Huber and Jessie's direction and were coming upon the Kachina Temple. Their time was short.

Hannah turned her back to the Brotherhood and focused her attention in front of her. Soon they had reached the summit. Lying faceup in the tattered remnants of sixteenth-century Spanish garb was a skeleton she had to assume was Esteban. Behind him were several weapons molded to their positions in the stone: a spear, a sling, a club with sharp diamond edges, and a golden vase.

"He who seeks the Golden Staff must choose the deadliest of all weapons," Hannah repeated.

"Shoot, all of these look pretty deadly except that vase lookin' thing. My vote is for that club. Can you imagine gettin' hit upside the head with that, Rico?"

"Yes, Cowboy, I see your point, but I believe the spear to be deadliest of these objects."

"No, something is off. The sling, spear, and club are all equally deadly. Why would Dorado put a vase with these?"

"Probably just to mess with us," Scott said. "C'mon, we don't have much time here. Grab the club!"

"I wonder what's in the vase."

"Poison, perhaps?" Alejandro said.

"Yes, that would be deadly. Or maybe a disease." Hannah's eyes widened. "If that were the case, then the vase would be more deadly than any of those. Does that make sense?"

"Nothin' you say makes sense," Scott said, then looked over his shoulder.

The Brotherhood's men were now traversing the second island.

"But I trust ya, so grab it!"

"But if I'm wrong, we'll end up like Esteban!"

"It won't matter in a few minutes when those guys catch up to us, will it?"

"Okay, here goes," Hannah said and stepped forward.

Taking a huge breath, she quickly swiped the vase out of its spot, closed her eyes, and waited. When nothing happened, she exhaled.

"You must'a been right! I'm still standin' here and ain't got no holes in me."

In the hollowed out space beneath where the vase was, there was a row of six squares. All were blank except the fifth one, which contained the symbol of a snake.

"It's a snake! We have the key! C'mon, let's hurry and meet Huber and Jessie!"

HUBER AND JESSIE SPRINTED toward the rendezvous point, a small rectangular landing sandwiched between the islands containing the Temples of Life and Quivira. Almost running parallel to them across the water over the bridge, Huber observed Hannah, Scott, and Alejandro running to meet them. From the rendezvous, they would follow the bridge that narrowed into a small walkway to the center island where *El Templo del Dorado* awaited. Huber just hoped his sister and the others had been successful in obtaining the necessary keys.

They reached the rendezvous point at about the same time.

"Were you able to find the keys?" Huber panted.

"Yes, we have them," Hannah replied. "It wasn't easy!"

"I bet you didn't have to die inside a coffin!"

"What?"

"I'll catch you up later. We gotta go!"

The masses of the Brotherhood were nearing, hemming them in from both sides.

"Let's get to it then!" Scott called out, and he took the lead and galloped toward the main island.

"Wait!" Hannah cautioned. "What does Niza say to do next?"

Jessie pulled out the next entry.

El Templo del Dorado

We reached the final temple of Cíbola, that of El Dorado. To gain access to the inner chamber where he and the Golden Staff reside, we had to use all of the keys we obtained from the sentinels and their order. The entrance inside was located nearly halfway up the pyramid.

Once inside, we faced many traps and obstacles. Upon reaching Dorado's inner chamber, I was the only survivor. I thought upon Esteban and all of the other lives that had been lost to find the Golden Staff. Staring upon El Dorado's golden form and the power within his hands, I was tempted to take it for myself. However, I could not bring myself to touch the evil gift. I knew the power of the Golden Staff would bring nothing but ruin and destruction upon the nation that possessed it and the world. With a heavy heart, I turned my back on the staff and made my way out of the city.

I write this entry outside of the entrance to the caves. Coronado will want to know what happened to all of my men. I will do everything I can to keep this power out of his hands.

My journey is at an end and so is my diary. If some unfortunate soul should happen upon my writings and seek this quest, I beg him to detour and save his soul.

Fray Marcos de Niza
April 17, 1539 anno domini

"That's everything," Jessie said.

"Sorry, Fray Marcos," Huber said to the air. "It's too late to turn back now."

He guessed they had maybe five minutes before the Brotherhood would catch up and overtake them.

They trekked the remainder of the way over the bridge that led them to the bottom of the massive pyramid. There was a shadowy space about halfway up the pyramid containing columns. Huber guessed that was the entrance to the temple Niza had referenced.

"Let's go!"

Sprinting up toward the doors, Huber quickly winded himself, but he couldn't afford to stop now. He briefly looked over his shoulder to see that the Brotherhood had reached the small rectangular landing that lead to Dorado's Temple. They were gaining faster than he thought.

"We don't have much time!" he shouted. "Quick! What are the keys?"

Hannah yelled back, "The moon goes in the first box, the sun in the second, and snake in the fifth. Were you able to find yours?"

"The skull goes in the third box, the feather in the fourth, and turtle in the sixth. I guess now we just have to figure out what it all means."

As they were speaking and climbing, Alejandro suddenly dropped unconscious and rolled a few steps down before coming to a stop. Everyone ran to him.

"What happened?" Huber asked. "Is he okay?"

Then he saw the red plumed dart sticking out of his neck. Another dart hit Scott in the arm, then a red laser-like dot focused on Jessie's shoulder followed seconds later by a dart sticking out of it. Within seconds, both Scott and Jessie slumped on top of the steps. Huber looked down and could see that Matón and his goons were nearing the bottom of the pyramid and were within firing range. Huber wondered why he could not see Fausto or Susurro. Perhaps they were in the back of the company playing it safe, as would be typical of the two.

"What do we do?" Hannah asked.

"We have to keep moving."

"And just leave them here for the Brotherhood? We can't do that!"

Huber shook his head, confused. "We're going to join them if we don't move!"

A red dot appeared on Huber's arm. He quickly jumped up and the dart whizzed by, crashing into the golden steps and shattering.

"C'mon!" Huber urged his sister and pulled her upward.

Seeming to agree they had no choice but to leave the others or lose everything, she followed her brother up the steps. Just before they reached the door, Hannah let out a quick yelp. Huber looked back to see her terror-stricken face. Turning around, he could see a dart sticking out of her shoulder blade. He yanked it out, but it was too late. Her eyes began to droop.

"Hurry, Huber. Get inside," she said, before dropping on the step and passing out.

Huber didn't have time to do anything but run. Finally, he reached the middle of the pyramid and its shadowy alcove. Tucked away were two heavy doors similar to the gates that had greeted them at the entrance to the city.

However, Huber wasn't focused on the doors or anything else. His heart dropped and the breath went out of him. Standing between him and the doors was Juan Hernán Salazar, smiling broadly.

Huber gasped at seeing his old nemesis. "How did you . . . ?"

"When you first opened the gates to the city, I slid in

behind you all undetected. I figured I would allow you and your friends to find all of the keys and save me the trouble and danger. I've been hiding and waiting here for some time. Now, give them to me!"

"I won't!" Huber said. "Go ahead and kill me if you like!"

Salazar laughed heartily. "I don't want to kill you, Yoo-ber. After all, you possess the keys, I assume, or you wouldn't be here. But we're in quite a predicament, aren't we? The Brotherhood is at the bottom of the pyramid as we speak and will soon make their way up. Share with me the keys and I'll help you. Once inside, we can talk about where we go from there."

"If I don't?"

"Then the Brotherhood will surely overtake both of us before we get inside. Once your friends awaken, I'm sure they'll use their methods of extracting the keys. We're wasting time!"

Huber didn't know what to do. Salazar was right that the Brotherhood would be upon them any minute, and he would rather take his chances with Salazar than an army.

"Fine!" Huber said, and he revealed the keys and their corresponding positions to Salazar.

"¡*Excelente*!" the man said. "Come, let's work together. Over here."

Adjacent to the doors there was a mechanism of some kind—six hollowed out blocks. Below the empty spaces were dozens of symbols etched into retractable golden cubes. They were obviously Zuni symbols of some kind. Huber quickly scanned them searching for any of the symbols they'd discovered. He saw a crescent moon near the bottom and pulled it out of its spot and slid it into the first space.

"C'mon and help me or we won't have time."

Salazar worked to find the other symbols they'd identified as keys. He found the feather and placed it in the fourth space.

Huber found the turtle and placed it in the sixth spot. From their position inside the alcove, they were protected from the Brotherhood's sleeping darts, but not likely for long. Huber found the skull and quickly placed it in the third space.

Salazar grabbed the sun symbol and slid it into place within the second spot.

There was only one more to go—the snake which belonged in the fifth and final spot.

Huber looked over the remaining symbols and couldn't find it, though there appeared to be a spot missing a symbol.

"Where is it?" Huber panicked. "The Brotherhood is coming!"

"It's right here," Salazar said and pulled it from his pocket. "I saw it earlier and thought it looked pretty. I didn't know it was one of the keys." He smiled.

Salazar slid the snake cube into place. As he did, the doors clanked and creaked open.

"Quick! Take out the symbols. We need to lock them out!"

Salazar and Huber yanked out the code for the combination and put them all back in their random spaces below.

Together, they slid through the doorway. Huber and Salazar pushed with all their might and closed the doors just as the last sliver of sunlight outside revealed Matón's brutish face coming into view. The golden doors slammed and clicked shut, locking into place. Huber and Salazar were instantly enveloped in darkness.

CHAPTER •17•

HUBER STEPPED FARTHER INSIDE Dorado's Temple
with the dreadful feeling he'd never see the outside world
again. At this point it didn't matter. What mattered was
keeping the staff out of the Brotherhood's and Salazar's
hands. If he failed, the world would be changed unal-
terably for ill. If he succeeded, the same world would be
spared the Brotherhood's unlimited, unrighteous domin-
ion. That no one would ever know the sacrifice and pain it
took to keep this evil in check saddened him, but his feet
were resolute as he stepped over several large tiles toward
an ascending set of narrow steps, encapsulated within a
corridor. Salazar kept pace beside him, and Huber made
sure to keep an eye on him.

The battery-powered lantern in Salazar's hand illuminated the path a few paces ahead. Just as the rest of

the city, the inside structure appeared to be constructed in solid gold. The steps ascended upward into darkness. On both sides of the upward path were ornately engraved walls, and there was a shallow ceiling above. The glyphs carved into the walls likely told of Uhepono's deception and the downfall of Lonan, who became El Dorado, but Huber didn't have time to inspect them closely. He wasn't surprised at the sound of grinding gears as he put his weight on the first step.

"What did you do?" Salazar hissed.

Huber closed his eyes and waited for some terrible booby trap to do its work. Maybe a huge boulder would fly down the steps like something out of an Indiana Jones movie, but the sound passed and he still stood. Perhaps the booby trap had malfunctioned. Then, turning backward, he realized his gut had been right. Even if he retrieved the staff, Dorado had ensured he'd never gain access out of this chamber.

Just a few feet from where he now stood, the large blocks of gilded tile he and Salazar had walked on had flipped, rotated, and dropped from the floor, reveal-ing a chasm of sharp, stalagmite-like spikes jutting out of a shallow pool of water. He brought the lan-tern toward the ten-foot wide chasm standing between himself and the archway that led out of the chamber. The barbs and spikes below were fashioned from bone, rock, and metal. Within the death trap, Huber gasped at several skeletons entwined within the briar. The corpse directly below him had met a particularly grue-some fate. A spike protruded directly through its eye socket. The other socket looked up at him as if pleading for help. Some of the man's clothing was still intact, and Huber knew they weren't from the 1500s.

"It's Joshua Cain," Huber mused. "He almost made it."

"Who?" Salazar barked angrily.

"Someone who beat us here by a hundred years," Huber said dryly.

Huber guessed the other skeletons were part of Niza's expedition, but he wondered how those earlier explorers ended up down in the pit. Maybe someone ahead of them had taken the first step and they had the misfortune of standing in the wrong place at the wrong time. Steeling himself, Huber took a breath and turned from the grisly sight back toward the corridor.

"Too bad you weren't standing a little farther behind me," Huber said to Salazar.

The man smirked. *"Así es, jóven.* Still, I prefer that you go first." He motioned upward.

There was no turning back now. Huber ascended the first few steps and no other sounds came. After traveling up twenty steps, he could see the corridor plateau into a platform ahead. With as much caution as he could muster, Huber approached the final steps. He brought his foot down on a stair and immediately knew it would likely be his last. The grinding sound resumed, and before he could think, the steps beneath and behind them fell flat like dominos. Huber and Salazar tumbled to their sides and were instantly accelerating toward the spike-laden death trap waiting to devour them below. The lantern rolled in front of him, lighting the way and casting shadows of their final descent down the chute. Huber clawed, kicked, and scratched at the floor and walls, but everything was flat and smooth. It was impossible to gain a foothold. There was absolutely nothing to latch onto or stop their downward trajectory.

After all he and his companions had been through, Huber couldn't believe it was going to end in such a grisly and unfair manner. He watched helplessly as the lantern bounced over the edge, casting a warm glow upward before being smashed against the spikes below. Huber's world plunged into darkness, but he kept speeding forward. He screamed in terror as he visualized himself being impaled like those who had gone before. What was more terrifying however was the thought of dying alone in this dark, forsaken place; to be forgotten until some other explorer looked upon his remains and wondered who he had been. At least Joshua Cain would have some company.

As he cried out for divine intervention, he pitched onto his belly and felt his knees slide over the edge, but he didn't fall. Something had stopped him. Huber's feet dangled over the abyss, but his arms were secured.

It was at that moment he realized someone had caught him before he plunged into the death briar. The person who held him grunted and pulled him up over the edge of the precipice. Then Huber felt his feet touch solid ground as he collapsed in a heap into Salazar's arms, struggling to keep himself from sobbing and hyperventilating.

"You saved me," he breathed to the figure in the dark. "How did you stop yourself from going over with me?"

The sound of a sparked lighter echoed through the chamber, and a small flame dispelled the surrounding darkness. Salazar's face materialized.

"This," he said and held up what remained of his treasured knife. Its edges were chinked and it barely held together. "I dug it into the floor to slow my descent. It slowed me enough to keep from falling over the edge."

"So why didn't you just let me go over?"

"Because, Yoo-ber, if you are going to die today, it will be by my hand, not in some death trap that denies me the satisfaction."

Huber looked into the face that had haunted his dreams and filled him with fear on more than one occasion. Juan Hernán Salazar stared back at Huber with his bluish white eye. The fact that his foe had just saved his life after Huber almost ended his was throwing him for a loop and causing some guilt.

"Yeah, well . . . thanks."

"Do not thank me yet, *jóven*. By the time all is said and done, you may have preferred I let you join the others down below."

"One other thing. How did you get across the chasm with the bats after I cut the rope?"

"I survive, *jóven*. Have I not proven that much already? You cannot rid yourself of me so easily. After your group left me to die, I clawed my way to the top of the ledge. I heard voices coming, so I hid myself among the rocks. Shortly thereafter, the Brotherhood came marching through, hundreds of them. Needless to say, with their resources, they were able to secure a walking bridge in a matter of minutes. I shadowed the end of their lines. When one of the stragglers stopped to rest, I knocked him unconscious and took his uniform. Within his mask, I was well concealed. I gradually worked my way up to the front lines. When the army stopped to take a rest, I sunk away to the shadows, shed the uniform, and pressed forward as fast as I could. I caught up to you just as you opened the gates to Cíbola. While you were all *oohing* and *ahhing* over the city, I snuck past the gates and once again concealed myself among the ruins. I worked my way to this place and have been waiting. Feels like old times, doesn't it, *amigito mío?*" He laughed. "You know, I was afraid there may have been traps."

"So you let us be your guinea pigs!"

"In a manner of speaking, *sí*," he nodded. "However,

we are now both stuck here like rats, thanks to you." He pointed to the death trap on one side and the sloped corridor on the other. "We cannot escape either way."

"So I ask again, why did you save me?"

Salazar stared through Huber, showing no hint of emotion. His expression was cold steel. "I told you already. If you die, it will be by my hand. That, and I may need your assistance."

"What do you mean by that?"

"There may be a way we can still escape this place, *jóven*, but we will need to work together. Look at the passageway." He pointed to the chute he and Huber had just descended. "How wide do you think it is, wall to wall?"

"I don't know. Five or six feet."

"*Así es.*" The man clapped Huber on the shoulder. "Right!"

Huber instantly slapped his hand away.

"If we sit back to back and interlock our elbows," he went on, "I believe we can shimmy our way up to the top of the chamber."

"And what if it doesn't work and we end up losing our footing? We might not be so lucky next time we go sliding down the chute."

"Then at least we will go together." Salazar smirked and glanced at the death trap. "Better than starving here in the dark or waiting for the Brotherhood to finish us, isn't it?"

Huber couldn't argue. But how could he actually work in unison with this monster? The same man who had threatened his life and betrayed him time and again; the same man who only cared about himself; the same man who had killed Grandpa Nick. But what choice did he have? Salazar was right. The chute was probably just wide enough that they could scoot their way up along both sides of the wall if they sat back to back. A startling question surfaced in Huber's mind. "Wait! What happens when we get to the top?"

"What do you mean, what happens?" Salazar snarled. "We survive. Perhaps find the Golden Staff and a way out."

"And you just let me go? What's to stop you from throwing me down that slip-and-slide of death when we reach the top?"

In the faint flicker of the lighter, Huber noticed Salazar's face redden.

"I just saved your life, *jóven*."

"For your own gain. I know you well enough. As soon as we're up there, I'm as good as dead. How can I trust you?"

Huber noticed Salazar compose himself. "You can't trust me, *jóven*." A slight crack in Salazar's countenance evinced a grin. "The truth is I've grown quite fond of you, Yoo-ber. We are the same, you and I."

"We're not the same. I'm nothing like you," Huber spat.

"*Sí*, we are! Both of us are survivors. Both of us will

stop at nothing to reach our goals. Look how far we've come! We are the same. *Tesoro de los Muertos*, imprisonment at the Brotherhood's castle, journeying here to the Temple of El Dorado. Look around," he said, waving his arms. "There is no one else here save you and I. What does that tell you? I cannot promise what will happen when we reach the top, *jóven*. Fate has set us apart as equals; therefore, fate will decide who prevails, and fate will decide who gains possession of Dorado's Golden Staff."

"Maybe I'll just decide to sit here. Then neither one of us will get the staff."

Salazar continued grinning. "That is your choice. We can sit here and die together. But how long do you think it will be before the Brotherhood or someone else finds this place and takes possession of the staff?"

Huber said nothing but knew Salazar was right again. Huber could throw his life away to keep Salazar from getting the staff, but eventually someone like him or worse would find it. If Huber could keep the staff out of evil hands and hide it somewhere else or better yet, somehow destroy it, he believed it would be worth the risk.

"I see in your eyes that you agree with me."

Huber hesitated for a moment but then stared straight at Salazar. "Let's go. But I can't promise what will happen *to you* once we reach the top."

Salazar's grin widened.

"I would not have it any other way."

●   ●   ●

Halfway up the chute, Huber's legs were quivering with fatigue. With their elbows locked together and their torsos acting as one, it took constant pressure at odd angles to keep himself from losing his footing. The only relief came when it was his turn to shimmy up and let his weight rest on Salazar's back momentarily before the villain would repeat the gesture. Progress was slow, but they were moving upward.

"Almost there, young friend," Salazar wheezed. "Just a bit farther to the top. Tell me, Yoo-ber, how do you plan to defeat me once we reach El Dorado?"

"Wouldn't do me much good to tell you now, would it?"

"You cannot defeat me, young one. Both of us know this. However, I would like to know what you would do with the staff."

Huber bicycled himself up a few feet farther and rested a moment before responding. "If I couldn't destroy it, I'd take it back to the Zuni so they could re-hide it from people like you."

"Like me? Are you so naive? There are plenty like me among the Zuni as there are people like me everywhere. Not everyone is as noble as you and your friends," Salazar said as he scooted upward.

"Then maybe I'd take it to the middle of the ocean and drop it in," Huber replied and took his turn.

"And risk turning the ocean to gold? End the world? You cannot destroy the staff, *jóven*. It would corrupt you as easily as it would anyone."

"Yeah? I don't think you'll be around to see what happens, so no need to worry about it."

"Again, how will you defeat me, *jóven*?" Salazar repeated. "I am bigger, stronger, faster than you."

"The same way I defeated you at Dead Man's Treasure—outsmart you."

Salazar quit laughing and shuffled upward, purposefully putting more weight on Huber's back, causing him to grunt with strain.

"You are *not* smarter than me, *jóven*!"

Salazar released his weight and Huber shuffled upward and was suddenly out of the chute on flat ground. They had made it to the top! Huber heard Salazar clamber up behind him. The inner section of the chamber was pitch black. Salazar still had the lighter. The safest thing to do would be to get away from the man before he sparked it alight. Huber scrambled through the dark on his hands and knees and found the wall of the chamber. He hoped he didn't fall into some other trap by accident.

"Yoo-ber," Salazar whispered in the darkness. "It is a small room. You cannot hide."

Huber heard Salazar spark the lighter. Through the darkness, he could see the bluish sparks fizzle as the flame failed to ignite. The lighter seemed to be empty of fuel.

"Hmmm." He grunted angrily and threw the lighter to the ground. "No matter. I will find you, *jóven*. Darkness cannot stop me."

A different voice suddenly resounded through the darkness. "It may not find you. But we will."

Suddenly, the room lit up with torchlight. Huber shielded his eyes. When he removed his hands, he viewed a silver mask dancing in the light just a few feet away from him. King Fausto stood before them, adorned in the same ceremonial garb he had worn inside the throne room in Spain. The long flowing, red robe, rock-sized rings composed of jewels, black leather boots, and stainless steel conquistador-style helmet conveyed a militaristic royalty. Instantly, his loyal confederate, Susurro, emerged from the shadows. He was also dressed in his royal clothing and steel helmet. He tased Salazar with some sort of device, sending him into convulsions.

"We've been waiting," Fausto said.

"How did you get up here?" Huber asked.

In his free hand, Fausto held up the weathered, leather journal of Fray Marcos de Niza.

"We had already figured out the general location of Cíbola. We knew it was within these caverns. We just didn't know exactly where. The journal was useful in helping us obtain the keys and avoid certain . . . missteps on our way. I had Matón and a legion of my best men wait for you all to enter the caverns and then follow up your rear just to ensure you didn't try to escape."

"So you're saying we walked into a snare the minute we stepped inside Carlsbad Caverns?"

"Afraid so, though I'm surprised you made it this far without Niza's diary, but I was secretly hoping you would."

Salazar was now stirring on the ground. Susurro had bound his wrists behind his back while he was recovering from the electric jolt.

"Ahh, Juan Hernán ... or Halcón. What do you prefer to be called these days, my pathetic friend?" Fausto flicked his wrist. "No matter. Would you both like to meet El Dorado?"

Fausto stepped to one side. As he did, the torchlight glinted off a golden statue sitting on a throne. The skull's expression was even, his chest bare save for an elaborate necklace and breastplate, and his head adorned with long, exotic feathers, which still retained their vibrant colors. His face was exactly the way it had appeared on the doors leading to Cíbola. Huber had to remind himself that it was not a statue, that it was actually a man. More specifically, it was Lonan, who had been granted the Golden Staff by the demon Uhepono. The man who had turned his city, its residents, and himself to gold with its power. The Golden One—El Dorado.

Within his grasp was a short staff, its appearance just longer than a cane. Dorado's left palm was facing up and resting upon it was the long end of the staff. His right hand was cupped over the tip of the staff, which contained an amber stone, almost glowing in the faint light of the chamber. It was shaped and contoured like a gleaming, translucent egg. Huber couldn't help but be entranced by Dorado's otherworldly presence. He wondered why the Brotherhood had yet to remove the staff from his hands.

Fausto motioned for Huber to come forward.

"You beat us," Huber admitted grudgingly. "Why haven't you taken it?"

Fausto sniggered. "That's why I was hoping you would make it. Come forward, Huber Hill," he beckoned. "Do you not recall all of the many traps you encountered along your way? I can only imagine what El Dorado has in store for the one who actually dares take his staff. You will remove it. If you survive, you will hand it over to me."

Huber almost laughed out loud. "Yeah right. Why would I do that? Maybe I'll just turn you to gold where you stand."

Fausto lifted his torch higher, casting the light's circumference a few feet farther. Toward the back of the chamber, behind Dorado's throne, the light revealed something Huber had not expected to see. Situated on their knees, blindfolded and gagged, were Huber's and Scott's parents. They were struggling, but their bonds were tight.

"If you don't turn the staff over to me, you will watch as I send your mother and father down that chute to their deaths right before your eyes."

Huber's father, Robert, was able to spit out his gag.

"Don't you dare help him, Huber! Don't do anything he says!"

Susurro scurried to the man and quickly plugged up his mouth again.

Fausto then turned his attention back to Huber. "So, what will it be?"

Huber exhaled and mulled it over. He had no choice. "I'll do it," Huber said.

"Great!" Fausto said. "Susurro, bring the parents over here just in case our friend tries to pull something."

One by one, Susurro dragged Robert, Ellen, and Brad just inches from the top of the chute.

"If you hesitate in giving me the staff, they go over the edge. If you try to attack us, they go over the edge. If you even look at me funny . . . do you understand, Hill?"

Huber nodded. "I understand."

"Good, then go ahead." He motioned toward the golden throne.

Huber approached the throne, Dorado's vacant eyes seeming to pierce his very soul. A million thoughts ran through his mind. He looked over and made eye contact with Salazar. His face carried an expression Huber had never seen the man wear before—*fear.*

"Yoo-ber," he said. "If we don't make it out of this, know that you were my most formidable foe."

Huber paid no mind to the man but turned his gaze forward.

Slowly, he ascended the steps leading up to the dais, which held the throne. Huber came face to face with El Dorado and wrapped his fingers around the end of the Golden Staff and closed his eyes. As he did, the face of El Dorado swirled in his mind, then came into focus. A white light burned within the skull's eye sockets and he opened his mouth. In the eye of Huber's mind, El Dorado spoke.

I am Lonan, son of Koli and Manakah. Who approaches my throne?

Huber answered in his mind, stating his name.

Why do you seek the staff?

Huber indicated with his thoughts that he desired to destroy it.

The answer seemed to please El Dorado, but Huber could feel the sadness and emptiness within the man.

The staff can only be destroyed by one who truly does not desire its power.

Huber asked what he should do.

Your motives and intentions must be pure. If they are, then you will be able to smash the stone and free us all from this place. Please free us!

Huber opened his eyes and slowly slid the staff from

El Dorado's hands. The staff weighed heavy in Huber's hands and the power within seemed to radiate and pulsate through his entire body. Huber tried his best to fight back the thoughts that instantly bubbled their way to the surface. With the staff, he was the most powerful person in the world! His imagination soared wildly at what he could do for himself, his family, and friends with infinite wealth. Pushing those thoughts aside, Huber focused again on reality and recalled the words of El Dorado that only someone with pure intent could destroy the staff.

"Very good, Hill," Fausto said, shaking Huber from his hypnotic status. "Now, hand it to me."

Huber knew if he didn't try now, he'd likely never have another chance to destroy the staff. Mustering his courage, he raised the Golden Staff high in the air.

"What are you doing?" Fausto shouted, panicked.

Huber closed his eyes and brought the amber tip crashing down upon the floor.

To his dismay, the tip of the staff bounced off the tile and didn't break. Instead, the tile in the floor underwent a metamorphosis. A golden spot formed in the center of the tile where the stone made contact. Seconds later, the spot sprouted filaments that spread to the edges of the tile. Huber's heart sank. Evidently, his heart was not pure enough to shatter the stone. He had wasted his one opportunity and likely forfeited his parents' lives in the process.

Everyone in the room watched with rapt attention the newly transformed tile in the floor.

Fausto then turned his attention back to Huber.

"Very noble of you, Hill. Susurro, send his parents down the chute, if you please."

Susurro giggled and pushed Huber's father toward the slope.

"No!" Huber shouted. "It's yours! Take it! Just don't hurt them!"

Huber tossed the staff to Fausto, who caught it with his right hand.

The leader of the Brotherhood exhaled in pleasure and gripped the staff tightly. Closing his eyes, he relished the moment.

"I've been waiting so long for this. Years and years. Finally, the Brotherhood of Coronado has prevailed. We will rule this world with strength and stability. The entire earth will call me King!"

"Our parents!" Huber shook Fausto from his trance. "You gave your word."

"That I did," the man said. "Susurro, bring them to me."

The diminutive king whimpered in dissatisfaction and moved Huber's father away from the chute and toward the center of the room. He did the same with his mother and Scott's dad.

"We now know how the staff works on inanimate objects like a tile, but how about living beings?"

"No!" Huber screamed.

His mother stared at him comfortingly and nodded to him that it would be okay.

Huber turned toward Fausto. "You promised! Please don't hurt them!"

"I'm sure it won't hurt at all." He laughed wickedly.

Huber watched helplessly as Fausto tapped Scott's father on the head with the staff. A gold spot appeared and slowly spread over his face just like it had on the tile, forever freezing his contorted expression of fear. It took mere seconds for the filaments to cover his entire body. He was now a statue, similar to the ones Huber had seen throughout the city. Huber's heart sank as he wondered how he would tell his best friend what had happened to his father.

"Now for the Hills," Fausto said and moved toward Huber's dad.

"Please!" Huber pleaded. "Don't! I'll do anything!"

Ignoring his pleas, Fausto tapped Huber's dad on the shoulder. The gold spot appeared and spider webbed out over the remainder of his body. It was like a terrible nightmare from which Huber couldn't emerge.

"Finally, Mrs. Hill." Fausto turned toward Huber's mom.

Huber fumed up at Fausto. "I swear I'll kill you!"

"Temper, temper."

Huber's mom spat out the gag and looked him in the

eye. "Don't look, son. Turn away. Know your dad and I will always be with you and Hannah. We love you."

Huber shook helplessly.

"Touching," Fausto said and gently tapped Huber's mother's hand with the staff.

As the gold spot began to weave its way up her arm, Huber closed his eyes and turned away. When he opened his eyes, his mother's warm eyes were still looking upon him, the tears forever solidified on her face. Huber went numb and dropped to the floor.

Fausto said in a cold and hushed tone, "Such is the fate of all who cross the Brotherhood, Huber."

Huber stared vacantly ahead, unable to formulate words.

Fausto continued, "We will soon show the world our newfound power. I can think of no better way than a live demonstration broadcast for the world to see. Huber, you will watch as I turn your friends to gold. Don't worry, you will join them as well afterward. Oh, and don't think I've forgotten about you, Juan Hernán. Can you imagine the fear? The reverence the world will have for us? Susurro, bind Mr. Hill, would you?"

Huber stayed on the ground, his eyes still riveted on his parents. It was his fault! He hadn't been able to destroy the staff. He had failed and let everyone down, the living and the dead. The staff was now in the hands of a madman. Susurro pushed Huber onto his side and bound his hands behind his back. He came face to face with Salazar, also bound and helpless.

Susurro slinked over to the wall and pulled a lever. The stairs that had fallen away in the chute rotated back into place.

Fausto looked upon the golden king and his throne, then bowed mockingly. "*Gracias, Rey Dorado. ¡Gracias por este regalo royal!* Thank you for this royal gift!" Fausto moved closer to Dorado and grabbed the skull though the eye sockets, pulling hard.

The skull came loose and Huber realized it was a mask. Beneath it lay El Dorado's true face; that of an old man etched with worry, regret, and disappointment. His eyes were closed as if he were deep in thought.

Fausto held the golden skull mask reverently in his hands. The king shed the silver mask and helmet, dropping them to the floor. Slipping the golden skull over his face, Fausto exhaled in triumph. "I am now the Golden King!"

Salazar made eye contact with Huber. "It appears fate has sided against both of us, *jóven*."

Huber said nothing.

CHAPTER
• 18 •

AS THEY MARCHED OUT of the gates leading from Dorado's Temple and down the steps to the plaza below, Huber could see that his friends and sister had awoken and were bound. Eagle Claw was badly beaten, but still standing, though bound as well. The expressions on their faces were grim. Huber couldn't bring himself to make eye contact. Hannah and Scott looked at Huber with pleading eyes.

"Huber!" Hannah shouted, obviously glad her brother was still alive. "What happened?"

"Our parents," he mumbled.

"Where are they?"

Huber slowly brought his gaze to meet his sister. "Inside the temple."

"They okay?" Scott asked. "How come they're not with you?"

His tongue seemed bound to the roof of his mouth, and Huber was afraid if he uttered a word, he would break down, but his face could not hide his feelings. He simply shook his head. "Fausto touched them with the staff," he said, still in shock.

Hannah and Scott stood agape. Tears streamed down Hannah's cheeks. Scott dropped to his knees, then looked up in red-hot anger as Fausto made his way down the temple. He was so enraged, it seemed no words could escape his mouth.

Matón and his legions erupted in a loud cheer as they witnessed their masked emperor stepping toward them with the Golden Staff in hand, his royal robes floating down the steps.

Huber couldn't see any scenario that would deliver them from their dire circumstances. He and Salazar were lined up alongside the other prisoners.

Huber turned toward the group. "I tried to destroy it, but I couldn't. I wasn't worthy enough."

They were cut off as Fausto addressed his troops from the bottom steps of the pyramid.

"¡Hermanos mios, tenemos la victoria!" he shouted to loud cheers. "We are victorious! Soon we will step out of the shadows and rule this world as it should be ruled, with an iron—no, with a golden fist! As loyal servants to the Brotherhood, you will all be rewarded beyond your wildest imaginations!"

The legion of men erupted. Huber guessed there must have been close to three hundred men standing in the plaza surrounding the temple.

"Matón! Susurro! My fellow kings, come forth and kneel before me!"

The two lesser kings approached their leader and bowed to the ground.

"You have been faithful to our cause. You have worked and sacrificed much for this day. Without your assistance, this triumph would not have been possible."

"*Gracias, Rey Fausto,*" Matón growled.

"*Sí, gracias rey mío,*" Susurro said.

"Prepare now to receive your reward. A coronation of sorts!"

Suddenly, Fausto brought the staff down upon the head of Matón and just as quickly swung it toward Susurro, connecting with his shoulder before he could dodge the blow. Huber and the others watched in horror as golden spots appeared where Fausto touched them with the staff. The two men lurched forward, but their movements were almost in slow motion as they reached toward their king with grasping hands. The golden spots expanded and the men's joints stiffened. Within seconds, it was as if they'd been frozen stiff. Their entire frames were now statues of solid gold.

Fausto then looked upon his men who were grumbling uneasily at the turn of events.

"Know this, my soldiers! There can be only one king!"

The men's grumbling died down.

"Who is your king?"

"Fausto!" they cried out in one voice.

"From out of the darkness, we will go forth. Let us make way to the surface. The world is ours for the taking!"

● ● ●

The walk back toward the surface was the longest Huber could recall in his lifetime. Each step brought him, his sister, and his friends closer to doom. Their fate would be the same as all of the innocent souls who had been left behind in Cíbola, including his parents. The same souls Huber had failed to free. As they approached the Bottomless Pit, Huber observed that the Brotherhood had installed some kind of mechanized, flat elevator that hauled a dozen or so people up at a time. As they awaited their turn, Huber overheard some of the soldiers bragging about how they'd won a government contract through one of the Brotherhood's phony companies to rewire and upgrade the lighting systems within the caverns for the next few days. Carlsbad Caverns had been shut down to the public and rangers. The place was completely empty of visitors.

Huber and the others eventually took their turn on the makeshift elevator and were brought to the main level of the caverns. They marched past the familiar sites of

Mirror Lake and the Big Room, and it all seemed so long ago when they'd first entered even though it had only been a day. Hiking toward the massive entrance to the caverns, Huber saw the twilight bathe everything in a warm glow, but it held no hope. He was grateful that he'd at least see the sky and sunset one last time before being turned to gold. Plus he'd be with his family and friends, which was a semi-comforting thought.

Huber watched as Fausto and most of the legion marched out of the caverns ahead of them. A small contingency escorted them near the back of the group. As Huber stepped out into the daylight and into the amphitheater, his eyes burned and blurred. Slowly, his pupils constricted and his eyesight adjusted. He couldn't believe it! Lining the seats of the theater and the earthworks surrounding it were literally hundreds of people, armed to the teeth. They appeared to be mostly Native American. Toward the top of the auditorium, Huber recognized two faces in the crowd—Malia and Sunitha.

The two throngs of enemies stared each other down, waiting for a pin to drop. Fausto, standing at the head of his legion, raised the staff high in the air.

"I am Fausto! I have obtained the Golden Staff of Cíbola directly from the hands of El Dorado! I command you all to step aside! Do so and avoid bloodshed. My men are well trained, and those who stand in my way will share the fate of those within Cíbola!"

From the top of the auditorium, Sunitha cried out, "The Zuni will not step aside!"

To her right, a man raised his arms in the air. "The Ute will not step aside!"

Another person cried out somewhere in the crowd, "The Apache will not step aside!"

"The Navajo will not step aside!"

"The Tewa will not step aside!"

"The Comanche will not step aside!"

Huber surmised that Malia and Sunitha must have been busy summoning and uniting factions of the various tribes to assemble within the area. The Brotherhood's men outnumbered them, but not by much. Huber guessed that Fausto was kicking himself now for prematurely ridding himself of Matón and Susurro. Huber had heard the slightest hint of fear in the king's voice as he had issued his warning.

"Turn the staff over!" Sunitha called out. "And we will let you live!"

Fausto and the Brotherhood laughed in unison.

"Do you not realize the power I hold within my hands? Bring the Ute man Eagle Claw to me!"

A member of the Brotherhood shuffled Eagle Claw and forced him to his knees, his back to Fausto.

"No," Huber whispered to himself.

Fausto took the staff and tapped Eagle Claw on the shoulder.

Eagle Claw stared ahead stoically, not struggling against the transformation. In his last moment, he turned his gaze to Huber and the others, managing a slight grin before the gold spread over his face. Eagle Claw, the once mighty warrior, was now a golden statue.

An unsettling murmur traveled through the assembled crowd as the Brotherhood's soldiers let out an intimidating, unanimous shout of approval at Fausto's actions.

Huber's stomach turned inside him as he stared at Eagle Claw's kind, frozen eyes.

"Who will be next?" Fausto cried. "If you do not wish to share this man's fate, step aside!"

Huber looked upon the assembled crowd, and though he could tell they were shaken, none fled.

"Very well!" Fausto shouted. "My brothers! Aim your weapons!"

As he finished his sentence, the men leveled their firearms loaded with toxic darts toward the crowd, but just as they did, the nightly swarm of bats erupted from the cavern entrance, covering the sky in a momentary blanket of swirling darkness. Standing in their path were the Brotherhood foot soldiers. As they dealt with the surprise onslaught of bats, their opponents seized the opportunity and charged forward. Seconds later, the two forces crashed into each other as the bats dispersed into the desert. Fausto wielded the staff as a weapon, striking those who approached him with it, turning them to gold where they stood.

Still bound, Huber and the others looked on helplessly. Then, without warning, his bonds were cut. In the melee, Huber looked around to see who had freed him. Juan Hernán Salazar nodded and was moving to cut the bonds of the others, obviously having slipped his restraints.

"Why are you helping us?" Huber yelled above the din.

"I told you, Yoo-ber, if you perish today, it will be by my hand and no other!"

Salazar dug into his pocket and retrieved a mesh Brotherhood mask, slipped it over his face, and disappeared into the thick of the crowd. Huber guessed he was going directly for Fausto.

Huber realized if they ran forward, they'd be caught up in the heat of the battle. Fausto seemed to be using a dozen of his men as human shields as they formed a semicircle in his front and attempted to escort their king out of the area. As Fausto had indicated, his legion of soldiers were well trained and seemed to be gaining the upper hand. Huber witnessed many of their allies fall to the ground, knocked unconscious through blunt force or through the use of poisonous darts. As Fausto passed over them, he made sure to touch them with the amber tip of the staff. Huber knew the brave people who had assembled there to fight would need all the help they could get.

"We have to help them!" Hannah said.

"What can we do?" Alejandro asked.

"We have the element of surprise," Jessie said. "We can sneak up on Fausto. He's well guarded from the front, but there is no one behind him."

"If we all take him together, we can get the staff from his hands!" Hannah said.

"Sounds better to me than runnin'," Scott said.

"We have nothing to lose," Huber said. "Our parents are gone."

"Alejandro, Jessie, you still have family. Go back inside where it's safe."

"No," Alejandro said. "We will fight with you until the end."

Jessie took Huber's hand. "You are also our family."

Huber nodded. "Then let's take him down. For our parents and for Eagle Claw!"

● ● ●

Huber averted his eyes from the scores of golden bodies strewn over the ground as they caught up to Fausto. He knew if the self-proclaimed king escaped the theater, it was likely no one would ever get a chance to stop him again. Soon, they were twenty feet away from the man.

His back was to them as a half dozen goons formed a barricade ahead of him.

"Now is our chance," Huber said. "He won't see us coming!"

Collectively, they rushed the man. Scott, fueled by anger, exploded out in front of everyone and crashed his shoulder into Fausto's lower back. The king went sprawling forward, the staff flying from his hands and into the dirt. Huber and the others were right behind.

"Get the staff!" Jessie pointed to the object.

Huber dove for it, but before he could grab it, a Brotherhood soldier was on top of him. The perimeter of men around the king noticed what was happening and collapsed on the rout. Before Huber could do anything else, he and the others were detained by the king's guard as the battle around them raged on. The soldiers forced each of them to their knees as Fausto arose from the dirt, dusted off his jacket, then picked up the staff. While only his eyes were visible behind the golden skull, Huber could tell the guy was seriously ticked off.

"Well, I had hoped to delay this until the most opportune moment, but I suppose now is as good a time as any," Fausto said as he brought the staff forward and touched Jessie on her shoulder.

Her eyes widened in shock as she locked her gaze with Huber. Her mouth opened in panic as the gold transformation took hold; in moments, she was as motion-less as the others strewn about.

Huber watched helplessly as Fausto went through the group one by one. With the staff, he touched Alejandro, Scott, and finally Hannah, their faces frozen with the terror of their final moments. A numbness spread over Huber as he watched.

Fausto finally approached him. "Such is the fate of all who cross the Brotherhood," he repeated. "Are you ready, Hill?"

Huber smoldered and kept his gaze steadfast, look-ing forward into the metal face. He would not go out cowering.

Fausto slowly brought the staff toward Huber's face. Suddenly, one of his men interrupted him.

"*¡Rey Fausto!*"

The king turned toward his minion. "What is it!"

The soldier slammed Fausto in the face, knocking Dorado's mask to the ground. In another swift motion, the soldier kicked the staff out of his grasp. The sol-dier shed his mesh mask and Huber locked eyes with Salazar.

Juan Hernán snatched up the staff and swung it at the remaining king's guard. He connected with three of the six in one fell swoop, then picked up Fausto from behind and held the tip of the staff inches from his forehead. The other three, upon seeing what had happened to their comrades and king, backed away and raised their firearms loaded with darts.

"Wait!" Fausto shouted to his men as he arose. "Don't do anything!"

"I've been waiting for this, *rey mío!*" Juan Hernán whispered in Fausto's ear.

Fausto smiled hesitantly, his mask still feet away on the ground. "Come, my friend. Don't be foolish. We can share the power and rule the new world together."

"As Matón and Susurro ruled alongside you? *¡Yo pienso que no!*"

Salazar brought the staff to Fausto's forehead and gently touched him between the eyes, solidifying his last moment of looking upward for mercy. Those engaged in battle nearby looked upon the scene and momentarily ceased their quarrel, unsure of what to do now that their king had fallen.

Salazar stepped away and picked up El Dorado's gold mask, then held it up for everyone to see.

"*El Rey Fausto* has fallen!" he shouted. "Cease this battle!"

A murmur swept through the crowd and everyone stopped fighting as they stared upon Salazar holding the golden skull mask in one hand and the staff in the other. Everyone waited to see what would happen next.

Salazar donned the mask.

"I am your new king! I am El Dorado reborn! Those

who follow me will not be subjects, but partners. We will not seek to rule the world, but simply enjoy its spoils! We shall fill our cups to overflowing!"

The Brotherhood's men showered accolades upon Salazar.

"The Brotherhood is dead. Remove your masks!"

The many soldiers did so, revealing their faces.

Salazar then addressed the factions of the Native tribes. "Those who have assembled here to fight the Brotherhood, your task is done! The Brotherhood is dissolved and disbanded! The remnants of their organization will crumble away with the loss of their three kings. I have no quarrel with you. Go home and live in peace."

The tribal members looked upon each other uncertainly, many seemingly unsure of what to do, but no one fled the scene.

Salazar sighed. "Very well. Are there any here who dare challenge me?"

"I do," a frail voice called out nearby.

A break in the crowd revealed Pincho and Don Carlos, sporting his questing equipment and trademark rapier. The man looked wistfully upon his grandchildren in their solid states, then brought his gaze back to Salazar.

"Juan Hernán, you are my blood and family, but I will not allow you to take the Golden Staff of Cíbola into the world!"

Salazar chuckled. "*Tío mío*, I see you're still alive, Uncle . . . barely. And you will stop me?"

"No." he shook his head sadly. "I am an old man and in poor health."

"He just awoke from a coma, or he would put you in your place," Pincho said.

"Ah, the faithful squire," Salazar replied. "You should follow me, Pincho. You could be rich and drink all the fine wines of the world."

Pincho took a swig from a nearly empty Pepto bottle. "No thanks. I've got everything I need right here."

Carlos continued, "I cannot stop you, my nephew, but he will." He pointed to Huber.

Carlos tossed Huber his rapier and winked. Pincho then addressed Salazar and the crowd in a booming voice. "The graceful Don Carlos issues the following proposal. If Huber Hill is able to obtain the staff from you, you and your men will surrender. If he fails, we will all surrender to you and allow you to leave this place without further incident. What say you?"

Salazar addressed his new army. "My brothers! What do you think of this proposal?"

The crowd cheered their agreement.

"Very well! Should this boy defeat me, we will all surrender to your desires. However, should I prevail," Salazar addressed the tribes, "you will all be subject to me!"

Everyone surrounding Huber and Salazar made room for the two to duel as the sun set and amphitheater lights illuminated the area.

Behind the golden skull, Salazar stared Huber down and breathed, "It appears that fate has smiled upon us after all, Yoo-ber."

Huber took a breath, briefly closed his eyes, then assumed the stance that Carlos had taught him over the last month. Why the old man had entrusted a novice with this task, Huber wasn't sure. However, he knew one thing. Where he had failed everyone earlier, he would not fail this time.

Salazar stepped toward Huber with the staff and made a wide swing toward his head. Huber ducked just in time and jumped back, falling on his back on the concrete. Salazar's army laughed in derision. The man then brought the staff downward, but Huber rolled away before it connected and jumped to his feet. Huber watched in awe as the concrete square on which he had been lying morphed into gold.

"Close call, *jóven*." Salazar chuckled as he thrust the tip of the staff toward Huber's torso.

Using the sword, he deflected the tip of the staff away. However, the force knocked the sword out of his hands, and he watched as his weapon morphed to gold on the ground. Huber dove and picked it up in a summersault before Salazar could swipe him with the staff. The sword was twice as heavy now, and Huber knew it would be infinitely more difficult to wield.

Salazar swung again, and Huber deflected the staff with the golden sword. The force knocked Juan Hernán off balance, and Huber took advantage of the vulnerability, tagging his foe in the right thigh with the blade.

Salazar cried out in pain and dropped to his knee. Huber brought the sword at him again, but the man blocked his attack with the body of the staff and pushed Huber backward. Salazar thrust himself up onto his feet again and moved with a slight limp.

"Accept your fate, *jóven*," Salazar snarled as he marched toward Huber. "You have nothing to live for now. Your family is gone; your friends are gone."

Huber yelled out and charged Salazar. His foe dodged the thrust and used the butt of the staff to knock Huber in the chest. He then swung the tip around with force and brought it within inches of Huber's face. Using his blade, Huber blocked the staff and pushed with all his might as the amber tip edged its way toward his eye. Salazar's army was cheering madly as the tip inched closer and closer. Huber felt his strength diminishing as his arms shook with fatigue. Soon this world would end. He wondered if the transformation would hurt.

From the corner of his eye, he saw Carlos, Pincho, Malia, and Sunitha cheering him on. They believed in him.

"Push off! Push off!" Carlos cried out.

Huber realized that though his companions and parents were gone, he still had friends who were depending on him. From deep within, Huber found his strength and pushed away from the staff, breaking the lock. Both he and Salazar fell to the ground. While Huber's sword was heavy, the Golden Staff was larger and bulkier. Huber could tell his opponent was becoming winded. He decided to exploit the weakness.

"You think anyone would ever follow you as king? You'd be as much of a leader as you are a ballerina!" he taunted.

Salazar took the bait and charged forward, swinging the staff wide at Huber. He bounced to the side before it connected.

"You're weak," Huber continued. "You are a weak, selfish man. You think that mask and staff can hide who you really are?"

Salazar ripped the mask from his face and tossed it to the side. His face was sweaty, red, and angry.

"I'm glad I spared you earlier, *jóven*. It will be so much more satisfying to watch you die by my hand!" he yelled out and charged, all the while swinging madly.

Huber parried his blow with the forte of his blade, then swung behind Salazar and sliced his left hamstring.

Salazar cried out and fell to the ground, relinquishing his grip on the staff. Huber threw his sword to the side and bolted toward the object. Salazar, clutching his leg, saw Huber running for the Golden Staff and grabbed Huber's ankle before he reached the relic. Huber fell hard on his face and the wind went out of him. The staff was almost in reach of his fingertips, but Salazar was pulling him backward. Huber used his free leg to kick the man in the face. Salazar let go, and Huber scrambled forward, grasping the Golden Staff within his hands. Huber rolled to his back to see Salazar coming down upon him with what was left of his knife. Huber brought the tip of the staff upward as a defensive instinct and felt the weight of Salazar land upon it, the amber tip disappearing in his chest.

Impaled by the staff, Salazar released the knife and dropped on his heels, the amber tip buried between two of his ribs, near his heart. He looked down at the staff, then at Huber. He blinked fast and pulled the Golden Staff from his chest, planted it on the ground, and used it to rest.

A golden substance gurgled from his wound, and Huber realized that Salazar's blood had turned to liquid gold. It seemed he was being transformed from the inside out. As he took his final breath, he looked into Huber's eyes.

"Well done, *jóven*. My cup is . . . empty."

Salazar's eyes then turned to gold, followed by the rest of his body, his hands still clutching the body of the staff.

Carlos limped toward the scene, retrieved the golden skull, and approached his nephew. Misty-eyed, he slipped the mask back over his nephew's face to hide his final expression.

"Adios, sobrino mío."

The remaining tribal members surrounding the theater exploded in cheers. The Brotherhood army, having lost both of their leaders in the space of an hour, dropped to their knees and pleaded for mercy from their opponents.

Pincho, Malia, and Sunitha approached Huber, whose gaze was still riveted on Salazar.

"I knew you could do it," Malia whispered and clapped Huber on the shoulder.

Pincho shook his other shoulder. "Nicely done, my friend! Take a victory drink." He offered the last swig of his Pepto to Huber.

"You saved so many lives," Sunitha said. "Thank you."

Huber looked at Hannah and his friends in their golden states along with all of the warriors who had come to his aid. "I couldn't save everyone," he replied grimly.

As the various tribes escorted the Brotherhood soldiers from the amphitheater, Huber and the others stayed below, lost in contemplation as they stared at all of the golden forms of the fallen.

"It's all my fault," Huber said to the others. "If I had been able to destroy the staff, none of this would have happened."

He retold the events that had happened within Dorado's Temple and his vision of the Golden King warning him that only one who truly desired to destroy the staff and not gain would be able to do so.

"I thought my intentions were pure, but right before I smashed it, these thoughts crept in about all of the things I could do with it."

Sunitha rested her hand over Huber's. "You are human. It is in our nature to desire such things. Do you care about any of those things any longer?"

Huber shook his head. "No. Not at all."

"What do you desire more than anything else?"

"To have my friends and family back."

Don Carlos whispered, "Where a man's heart is, there is his treasure also."

"Huber," Sunitha said solemnly. "Take the staff and try again to destroy it."

Huber shook his head. "I told you I couldn't. It won't do any good."

"Just try."

Huber approached the golden form of Salazar. Reluctantly, he wedged the staff upward out of his golden grasp.

Huber took a breath, raised the staff high in the air, and brought it down upon the concrete. To his amazement, the amber stone shattered into thousands of pieces and the whole ground seemed to shake and moan, and then it stopped abruptly. The staff that held the amber tip in place turned to ash and floated away in the breeze.

"You did it!" Malia shouted and hugged him.

Huber stared in disbelief.

Sunitha smiled. "It took the experience of losing everything to set your heart right."

Huber nodded. "I just wish I could've set it right without paying such a high price," he said, looking at his friends and family.

"Hey, look!" Malia cried and pointed toward the area where the earlier skirmish had occurred.

In the semi-darkness, Huber watched, amazed, as some of those who had been turned to gold on the battle-field began to stir and then return to their natural state of flesh and bone, the gold melting away into nothingness.

Sunitha continued, "According to legend, once the staff has been destroyed, those good who were touched by its power will be released from its hold. The evil will remain as statues forever, a warning to those who seek power and riches to dominate others."

"So you're saying . . ."

Huber couldn't finish his sentence before he saw the golden layer covering his sister slowly retract and evaporate. She fell to the ground and began to breathe again. The same happened to Alejandro, Jessie, and Scott. They all arose from the ground groggily.

"Dude, what happened to us?" Scott asked, rubbing his temples.

"You got turned to gold." Huber laughed. "How did it feel?"

"I dunno. Don't really remember. I guess it's the same feeling you'd get if you were abducted by aliens or something."

"Yes, Cowboy, I agree," Alejandro said. "It could've happened to you and you wouldn't even remember it."

Hannah came forward and hugged her brother. "You destroyed it! It was like a dream, but I was watching as you did it."

Huber turned to Sunitha. "Our parents were turned down below! Does this mean they're alive?"

● ● ●

They'd all made the trek back down to the golden city and found their parents confused yet marveling at the city of Cíbola. Like lost tourists, they were using torches left behind by the Brotherhood to examine their surroundings. Everyone had embraced for several minutes before anyone spoke.

Huber and Hannah caught their parents up to speed on what had transpired on the surface.

Scott and his dad gave each other a strange handshake and talked about the fortunes they could make as tour guides of Cíbola.

Don Carlos and Pincho took it all in.

"*Magnífico*," Carlos uttered over and over. "I am so happy I was able to see this place! Pincho! Which adventure shall we embark upon next?"

"I think it is time to retire, your grace."

Carlos waved a hand in dismissal. "The day I retire is the day I die!"

Huber noticed that the many golden forms they'd encountered throughout the city had disappeared or turned to ash. However, Matón and Susurro remained where they were at the bottom of Dorado's Temple. Huber wondered if El Dorado was still sitting on his throne or if he'd paid what was required of him and been released from his solid state. He supposed he would never know. A group of strong men from Sunitha's tribe had carried the golden forms of Salazar and Fausto down below and placed them next to Matón and Susurro. As Huber looked upon the faces of his enemies, especially that of the masked Juan Hernán Salazar, he felt true pity and hoped that one day their souls would find peace as well.

Huber, Hannah, and the others looked back at Cíbola one last time as they reached the golden gate and wondered if any would ever rediscover the lost city. He certainly hoped not. Some secrets were best left undiscovered.

EPILOGUE

HEADLINES GRACED THE FRONT pages of international news sources regarding the downfall of a nefarious faction called the Brotherhood of Coronado, bent on imposing their will on the world. Upon raiding their headquarters at the Castle Alcázar de Segovia, officials had discovered decades of missing treasures stolen from around the world. The treasures had been returned to their places of origin or within museums.

In Carbondale, the newspaper had focused on upcoming events like the school carnival or the recent play *Peter Pan*. None of the town's residents had any idea that a handful of its young residents had played an integral part in the Brotherhood's downfall.

After the experience in Spain and New Mexico, Scott, Huber, and Hannah returned to school. There was a certain buzz around the school about the arrival of the new Spanish teacher, Mrs. Ramirez. None of the students or faculty seemed to know what had happened to Mr. Mendoza. Some rumored that he had taken another job, and others believed he had returned to Spain or had retired to a beach somewhere. Huber possessed the truth but knew no one would believe it even if he told them.

It had been many months since the events transpired in New Mexico. Huber and Scott remained the best of friends, and Hannah had found her niche with the athletes of the school. Huber greatly missed Jessie and Alejandro. They had returned to Spain with Carlos and Pincho shortly after their adventure in Cíbola. Jessie and Huber had stayed in touch through email, though not as often as Huber would have liked. Carlos had recently written the family a letter, expressing his intent to search for the Fountain of Youth with Pincho. Sometimes Huber had visions of rejoining his Spanish friends on another adventure, but knew he'd likely never do so again.

● ● ●

It was a normal day at school when Huber received a shock. It was May, and there was only one month of school left. He and Scott were eating lunch when Hannah plopped down next to them. It seemed like it had been a long time since they'd all sat and talked together.

They made small talk for a few minutes before the vice principal entered the lunchroom, accompanied by two others. Huber couldn't believe his eyes. It was Jessie and Alejandro.

Jessie and Alejandro looked around the room, discovered their friends, and immediately ran to them and embraced. Scott even kissed Alejandro on both sides of his face as was the custom in Spain. He didn't care about all of the laughs that ensued around the room.

"Good to see ya, Rico!"

"You too, Cowboy!"

"What are you guys doing here?" Huber asked.

"The International Study Abroad Program." Jessie laughed. "We were selected to travel abroad. Of course, as you know, my *abuelo* is the head of the program." She winked. "We decided to come here to Colorado and study, if that's okay? We just need to find a family to host us."

"I think we can find a place for you to stay," Hannah said.

"How long are you here?" Huber asked.

"A month," Alejandro replied.

Huber couldn't believe the good fortune and thought about all of the things they could see and do with their time together.

"We expect a good time." Jessie smiled.

"And entertainment," Alejandro added.

"You've come to the wrong place then," Scott answered. "Nothin' exciting ever happens round here."

"We thought perhaps we could go camping up in the mountains."

"And you could take us to the place you found *Tesoro de los Muertos*—the Dead Man's Treasure."

● ● ●

Two weeks later, the three of them notified Eagle Claw that they were going up to Mt. Sopris through the Roaring Fork Canyon on a visit. He said he understood and they would not be bothered, but to remember to leave everything undisturbed. As they took the trail from their earlier adventure and followed the map from Huber and Hannah's grandpa, they laughed heartily as they reminisced on earlier days. Talk of Salazar, the Brotherhood, and Cíbola was kept to a minimum. The mountains themselves seemed to have stayed exactly as they'd left them, a feast for the eyes. The river still sang its beautiful song. The jagged, rocky cliffs still towered above the world, and the trees still bestowed their intoxicating aroma upon their olfactory senses. The fact that some things never change brought Huber a sense of comfort.

They made it to the clearing by the waterfall at the end of the first day. Scott and Hannah decided to take a walk while Huber built the fire. They snuck behind the waterfall and found their names still etched in stone, along with some newer graffiti. Early the next morning, they arose at dawn and made it to the mine at Dead Man's Treasure around ten, remembering the location of the skull hidden in the rock. When they reached the entrance, it was once again overgrown with ferns, vines, and grass. After clearing away the foliage, they tolled the bell thirteen times and ventured inside. Surprisingly, the mine was still holding up pretty well. This time they were prepared with lanterns, oxygen, and first-aid kits. Upon reaching the end of the cavern, they re-discovered the treasure. Eagle Claw and his friends had returned the treasure chests just as they'd left it earlier. However, all of the Spanish corpses had been removed. Eagle Claw mentioned their bodies had been there long enough and had received a proper burial. When Huber opened up the center chest, his grandpa's letter remained undisturbed for any new explorers who dared venture inside the mine.

As they prepared to depart the mine for the final time, Huber heard Hannah say something.

"What was that?" he asked.

"Oh . . . nothing," she answered.

"Tell us, Hannah," Jessie pleaded as she took Huber's hand in hers.

"I was just remembering something in Grandpa Nick's letter."

"What about it?" Huber asked.

"'Treasures . . . where neither rust nor moth doth corrupt, nor thieves break through and steal,'" Hannah quoted.

Everyone nodded their heads in silent agreement, understanding now more than ever what the words truly meant.

As they exited Dead Man's Treasure and neared the end of the canyon, they walked along a lazy stream and conversed further. They talked about plans for college. Where would they live? Would they join a fraternity? What would life be like living on their own? The future was so exciting. Perhaps they could take a year and study in Spain, or Alejandro and Jessie could study in America.

Huber became crestfallen as he realized they had just a couple more weeks before Jessie and Alejandro returned to Spain. "How long do you think it will be before we all see each other again?" he asked.

"Probably a couple of years," Jessie answered honestly. "It'll give you and Scott some quality bro time anyway."

"True, but you'll probably forget about us all in that amount of time."

"Never." She winked.

Continuing forward, Scott and Alejandro vied for Hannah's attention as usual. However, the serene atmosphere of the mountains overpowered their obnoxiousness. The sun was setting, splashing an array of spectacular color across the sky, reflecting off the slow, meandering stream. Up ahead, movement caught his eye. Turning, Huber stared in disbelief at the sight.

"Hey! Look!" Huber yelled excitedly as he pointed to a rocky ledge, hovering above them beneath a purple horizon.

There, alongside the edge of bluff, hobbled a one-eared cougar.

Huber thought of his Grandpa Nick and knew nothing was ever lost or truly forgotten.

Acknowledgments

DOES ANYONE READ THESE things? If you are, let me say thank you for investing the time and effort to read one of my books. I hope it was worth your time and you enjoyed it. I am grateful to the readers of the Huber Hill series. Your kind words, reviews, and support were essential to me as an author over the last few years.

It's strange saying good-bye to Huber, Hannah, and Scott. I've loved getting to know them as characters. The story started as a small seed of inspiration and grew into something much larger than I could have anticipated. I'll miss them.

More than anyone, I owe thanks to my wife, JulieAnn, who has been unwavering in her support of me as an author and, more important, as a husband and father. She is my anchor through the storms of life, and I love her so much. She's also a great editor! Since beginning the series, I've become a father of two amazing kids. The privilege of fatherhood outweighs everything. Daniel and Lucy, I'm honored and blessed to be your dad. Maybe one day you'll take one of my books to school and say, "My dad wrote this . . . and he's tougher than your dad."

I owe many thanks to Cedar Fort Publishing for picking up the series. The cover art, design, and editing have been wonderful. Specifically at the organization, I thank Angie Workman, Melissa Caldwell, and Kelly Martinez.

I am grateful to family and friends who have been supportive and advocates of my work: my mom (Cindy), who has always believed in and encouraged me, Jack, my brother Kirk, Michiel, Madison, Bob, Cindy, Justin, Jeanette, Ray, and Granny HaHa. I owe a specific thanks to Dean Nielson for our late night collaborative sessions on concept art and story elements. And I can't forget Jaxin and Malorie, my biggest fans.

As the series comes to an end, I hope this is just the beginning and there will be many more stories to come.

Thanks again to you, readers, for sticking with me. It means more than you know.

Discussion
Questions

1. *As Huber and the others trekked across the ocean, Huber discovered that he had a knack for sword fighting. What hidden talents have you discovered about yourself? How does a person go about finding his or her strengths?*

2. *At Carlsbad Caverns, Ranger Mike points out that one of the stalagmites was purposefully broken by a patron. This angers and saddens Huber and Hannah. How can we protect our natural wonders and teach others to be respectful toward them?*

3. *As the group enters the cave system to find Cíbola, they only do so with proper equipment and support. Why is it important to be prepared when going into nature, whether outdoors or underground?*

4. *Halfway through the story, Huber is confronted with a difficult choice when Salazar tries to cross the chasm. His decision angers Jessie. Do you think he made the right choice? Why or why not?*

5. *At the end of the story, Huber is able to destroy the staff only when his heart is in the right place. How do you interpret this quote, "For where your treasure is, there will your heart be also"?*

About the Author

B. K. BOSTICK RESIDES among the magnificent Rocky Mountains. In addition to writing, he has spent his career in education. He earned his bachelor's degree in psychology from the University of Utah and his master's degree in psychology from Utah State University. He has worked as a teacher, after school program coordinator, and teacher mentor, and he currently loves working for the Open High School of Utah. In his spare time, he enjoys eating Cheetos and watching old episodes of the *Twilight Zone.*

0   26575 10988   7

SIETE TEMPLOS
DE CÍBOLA

Kachinas

Muerte

Vida

MORGANTOWN PUBLIC LIBRARY
373 SPRUCE STREET
MORGANTOWN, WV 26505